THE FACTS KEEP GETTIN' IN THE WAY OF THE STORY

WILD AND WOOLY TALES FROM THE HISTORY OF ARIZONA AND THE AMERICAN SOUTHWEST

BY MICHAEL COYOTE PEACH

Published by Sedona Heritage Publishing, held by the Sedona Historical Society, Inc.
www.sedonamuseum.org
928-282-7038
Printed in the United States of America

Cover photo by Michael Peach
Rear cover photo by Janeen Trevillyan

Photos by Michael Peach unless otherwise noted.

To Jane and Zachary
with all my love.
You make it all possible.

Acknowledgements

Bill Levengood, chairman of the Sedona Historical Society's Publication Committee, approached me following one of my museum performances and asked if I'd like to have my work in print, and, while most of the poems and narratives were already written, his question marked the beginning of a two year journey of writing, researching, and assembling much of what follows here. He also took responsibility for formatting the text. Thanks, Bill!

Special thanks are due to Ray Anderson, Cynthia Batchelder, Mary Bowers, Ruth Clem, Jim Eaton, John Foglton, Patty Fox, Valerie Girard, Kathie Hamblen, Fran Levengood, Ron Maassen, Joan Miller, Morna Paule, Donna Pratt, Carol and Dave Thomas, Mary Wyatt, and the many dedicated SHM docents for their assistance in myriad forms. I am also indebted to the late Sherman Loy, Edith Smith Denton, and Sallie Petriccione for their skepticism, wisdom, and smiles.

I am very grateful to my friends and fellow northern Arizona authors Scott Baxter, James Bishop Jr., and Gary Every for taking the time to review and provide feedback on this work. I am humbled and honored by their endorsements.

This book would not have been possible without the unflagging support and encouragement of two very special women. My wife Jane has not only been a loving and tolerant helpmate and an invaluable source of feedback and honest criticism, but has on more than one occasion used her computer expertise to retrieve work I managed to send into the abyss of cyberspace. Janeen Trevillyan, an officially designated Arizona Culture Keeper, has been the driving force tasked with everything from providing creative suggestions, to writing the introduction, and retrieving photos from the museum archives. This book represents only a small fraction of her tireless work in preserving Arizona's history. It is a tremendous honor to have the support of these women, and I have endeavored to create something worthy of their respect.

My special thanks to Clinton and John Gray, grandsons of Tuffy Peach, for sharing stories and memories of their late grandfather, and providing me with a previously-unpublished photo of "America's last pony express rider."

I am also thankful for the work of the various historians and authors whose works I have cited, and for the efforts of the children and grandchildren of the valiant pioneers who kept the stories of their elders alive. Their preservation of memories and stories of the past provides us the opportunity to learn from them.

About the Author

Michael Peach is a certified professional interpreter of cultural and natural resources. He is a member of the Arizona Humanities Speakers Bureau, a Certified Interpretive Trainer for the National Association for Interpretation, and has created programs in archaeology and living history for the Sedona Heritage Museum and other clients including the National Park Service, the United States Forest Service, Arizona State Parks, Northern Arizona University, the Daughters of the American Revolution, and various civic and corporate groups. He is also a professional actor, director, and playwright with numerous stage and screen credits.

Photo by Zachary Peach

Introduction

I grew up in South Dakota, where one of the most famous cowboy poets, Badger Clark, was the state's Poet Laureate. Memorization and recitation of poetry was still at that time a dreaded (for the student!), but central part of elementary education. To this very moment, the almost singsong meter of Clark's "A Cowboy's Prayer" can transport me to my home on our family farm. Behind the words I can feel the unending prairie wind, hear the tune of a Meadowlark, and look out at a 360° view without another house.

> Oh Lord, I've never lived where churches grow.
> I loved creation better as it stood
> That day you finished it so long ago
> And looked upon your work and called it good.*

Maybe my personal history is one of the reasons that I have been so drawn to Michael Peach's poetry and stories over the tenure of our friendship.

But, no, cowboy poetry doesn't have to be written by cowboys, nor enjoyed only by cowboys. Newcomers to the genre might be surprised by the contemporary topics and viewpoints in today's writing, excellent examples of which are Mike's "A Bobcat Walked into a Cottonwood Bar" and "Sedona Sue". A cowboy's life has never been frozen in time, so why should cowboy poetry never change or adapt?

As an amateur historian, to understand something I have to know its ancestry. Historically, cowboy poetry grew out of a tradition of cowboys entertaining each other with tall tales and folk songs after long days on the trail. There is further surmise that they also had long hours in the saddle that needed filling. And, without a laptop or tablet in hand to record their deepest thoughts, observations of work, the environment, or of mankind (and womankind), their prose and song helped fill their time. Harkening back to my school days, I tend to gravitate to the proposition that the form may have its roots in the Victorian era when public recitations were much in vogue.

And, while cowboy poetry's modern and fairly recent renaissance might tend to make us believe that it is an oral tradition, from its' earliest days in the 1860s, it has been a favorite for publishing in trail town newspapers, national magazines and dime store paperbacks.

As someone who loves history, I appreciate accuracy but I can also appreciate being entertained. As a fine cowboy poet and story-teller, Mike's original work is just downright enjoyable. Thousands of people have heard Mike perform these pieces, but reading them allows one the leisure to digest deeper meanings, as well as to enjoy the delightfully self-conscious thematic word play embodied in poems like "Kissin' Jenny", "Keep a Close Watch on Your Heart", "Ira and the Bad Cook", and "The Man Who Killed Santa Claus". Cowboy poetry is rarely an academic's game. It is by tradition and by nature an accessible art form. From the simple honesty of "The Saga of John Munds" and "Tuffy's Christmas Ride" to the tongue-in-cheek satire of "If You Die in Arizona" and "The Hauntings of the Red Ghost", the collection you are about to read contains color and candor in Mike's view of the circumstances and characters he brings to you.

An old-time cowboy's life was hard and sometimes harrowing. They, for sure, must have lived by the adage: "Carpe diem".… or in cowboy poet vernacular: 'pluck the day'! But, heck! Living in our crazy modern world today isn't for 'sissies'. No matter if this is your first time or, like me, a return to this breed of composition, I invite you to 'pluck the day'. And, as Mike reminds us, don't let the facts get in the way of the story.

> Forgive me, Lord, if sometimes I forget.
>> You know about the reasons that are hid.
> You understand the things that gall and fret;
>> You know me better than my mother did.
> Just keep an eye on all that's done and said
>> And right me, sometimes, when I turn aside,
> And guide me down the long, dim trail ahead
>> That stretches upward toward the Great Divide.*

Janeen Trevillyan, Sedona Heritage Museum Historian

*Excerpts from Badger Clark's "A Cowboy's Prayer"

Author's Preface

Full disclosure: My parents did not give me the middle name Coyote. It does not appear on my birth certificate. I adopted it when I was nineteen. My friend Tim Yankee and I had gone backpacking in the Superstition Wilderness, about fifty miles outside of Phoenix. Both of us were born and raised in Phoenix, and had hiked and camped (and had experiences with altered consciousness) in the Superstitions many times prior to this, so we didn't let the fact that it was July – which would mean temperatures in the 120+ degree range – stop us from embarking on a three day adventure in that beautiful place. Believing ourselves to be immortal, we nonchalantly assumed we could carry three days' worth of water, and that all would be well. What we learned the hard way was that no matter how much water we could carry, in that temperature we would drink it all in one day. Fortunately, the fruit of the omnipresent prickly pear cactus was abundant, and we relied on this as a source of moisture, hiking during the twilight and night time hours. However, given the many tiny needles (glochids) which cover the skin of these fruits, the amount of seeds to be removed, and the large number of individual fruits it took to quench our thirst, it took us two days to hike back out. And in spite of our diligence at cleaning the fruits, our mouths were bristling with the tiny needles by the time we finally got back to Tim's truck. Not long after this painful experience, I learned that some of the indigenous native peoples of Arizona's deserts refer to a prickly pear fruit as a "coyote peach." Being already officially possessed of the last name, I took the other for my own, unofficially. To this day the name reminds me of that transformative experience, but it has not prevented me from behaving immaturely and/or stupidly on numerous other occasions.

I first saw Oak Creek Canyon when I was about six years old, and it made an indelible impression on me. I made a vow to myself that, if possible, I would one day try to live in the red rock area. In 1983 I finally moved to Sedona, having graduated from Northern Arizona University and spending several years earning a Masters degree and working in professional theater in southern California. It would be another couple of years before the dawning of Sedona's tourism renaissance, so I was holding down a variety of jobs while attempting to make ends meet, including working in a retail store, waiting tables in a prestigious restaurant, substitute teaching in Verde Valley High Schools (Sedona didn't have one yet), driving a taxi, writing and producing plays, and working as a "stringer" for Sedona's main newspaper, the Red Rock News.

By the mid-eighties, Sedona's tourism boom was underway, and my schizophrenic employment situation resolved itself into a triumvirate of

conducting archaeological tours for Time Expeditions, teaching theatre and honors courses at NAU, and performing roles in Sedona theater productions.
The late Warren Cremer mentored me in the archaeology of the prehistoric southwest and, as this remains an enduring passion for me, I am greatly indebted to him for that.

As the previous millennium was drawing to a close, I was approached by Cynthia Nasta, a coordinator for the Northern Arizona University Elderhostel program about creating a presentation on the territorial history of the Verde Valley. I ignored her initial request, but she was persistent and when she contacted me again several months later, she caught me at a time when I didn't have any other projects going, so I began to look into it. I've always been a lover of history, but I'm especially drawn to the quirky incidents that are most often ignored by mainstream texts. As I began to immerse myself in books like Pioneer Stories of the Verde Valley (compiled by members of the Verde Valley Pioneers Association), and The Arizona of Joseph Pratt Allyn (written by my former NAU history professor John Nicholson), I was immediately captivated by the heroism as well as the hubris and humor displayed by those who dared to take on the enormous challenges of carving out a life in what was one of the last and most remote corners of America's wild frontier. This study led me to discover and appreciate for the first time my own family's territorial roots in central Arizona.

My first Elderhostel history program was titled, Voices of the Verde. Thanks to the vision of Janeen Trevillyan, then president of the Sedona Historical Society, the program was offered monthly at the Sedona Heritage Museum. In the ensuing years, I have created other programs for my monthly shows at the museum – Mysteries of the Muggy-Own, Mischief on the Muggy-Own, and Arizona History and Hi-jinx (an official Arizona Centennial Event). I also wrote, directed, and performed in another of the museum's official Arizona Centennial events, Arizona's Constitutional Convention of 1910 – "You Are There". My association with the Sedona Heritage Museum is something I treasure deeply, and I am honored that my programs have found a home there. The continued support of Janeen and the rest of the museum staff has been invaluable in my continued explorations of this richly rewarding topic.

I believe passionately in the importance of remembering and learning from the past, and in storytelling as a primal means of imprinting on the human psyche. I find the genre of cowboy poetry to be a unique and highly entertaining vehicle for relating these stories. As a tradition, it certainly fits the subject matter, and it is being widely re-discovered across America. Some would stoutly maintain that it was never lost, but it is certainly reaching new audiences and gaining a renewed respect. Members of my audiences have frequently made comments like, "I never thought I'd enjoy hearing cowboy poetry!", and "What an entertaining way to learn history!" Some cowboy poetry purists may take exception to some of my chosen subject matter or to my use of "near-rhymes", but I make no excuses for what I have done in the name of telling these stories while maintaining a rhyme scheme. In spite of the satirical tone of some of these verses, it is my intention to honor the struggles, achievements, and even the foibles described herein. I subscribe to the philosophy that "cowboy" is a state of mind, but I am not now nor have I ever been an actual cowboy. I have eaten many a steak, but I have never punched a cow.

In the early, heady days of Sedona boosterism, there was a saying that one often heard bandied about at business gatherings: "Know how to make a million dollars in Sedona? Start with two million." Today one would probably need to increase that second figure significantly. This saying has a painful resonance to some of the fourth and fifth generation members of the Verde Valley's early pioneer families, many of whom now see shopping malls, resorts, and gated, multi-millionaire communities occupying their former homesteads, range lands, swimming holes, pleasure haunts, and scenes of the transcendent moments of their childhoods. Sherman Loy, who mentored me in my explorations of the valley's early history, once told me, "I chose to stay away from this valley for forty years, so I can't get too angry at what happened while I wasn't here." I'm sure other current descendents of these early families have also been forced to adopt a similar brand of philosophical stoicism. Change is, after all, inevitable, but in this regard, allow me to indulge in a story…

> There's an old joke about a guy who loses his way while driving through farm country. Fortunately, he sees a farmer leaning against the fence at the edge of a field just up the road. He pulls over and asks directions of the farmer, and while they are talking, he looks over the farmer's shoulder into the field beyond. Wandering about in the field is an enormous pig, really huge. And this pig has a wooden leg.

> Having gotten his directions, the man says to the farmer, "You know, there's just got to be one heck of a story about how that pig comes to have a wooden leg." "Oh, yeah," says the farmer. "That there's a prize animal. That pig saved my life once. Tractor went over on me down on the lower forty, and if that pig hadn't been there to pull me out, drag me back to the farm house and kick and squeal 'til the

help come out, I'da died out there. That pig saved my life. Prize animal." "Yeah," says the guy, "but what's up with that wooden leg?" And the farmer says, "A prize animal like that, you don't eat all at once."

We can look around our country and see we have any number of prize pigs, which we are carving up a leg at a time. But there's only so much pig, and our children and grandchildren haven't eaten yet.

Times have changed. Many more people have discovered the beauty of the Verde and have come to make it their home. The same can be said of our mountains, plains, rivers and shorelines, and even of our cities great and small. We cannot continue to meet our current challenges by appropriating, exploiting, and exhausting any available resource the way our ancestors and the Indians here before them did. Once these places of inspiration and rejuvenation have been sacrificed to development, they can never again be restored to their original, natural beauty.

So I call upon you – elders and members of the new generation, outdoor enthusiasts, visitors, resident citizens, architects and city planners, members of county planning and zoning commissions, and those empowered by positions within federal, state, and local governments – let's use our collective wisdom in treating this land as a resource we are charged with delivering to our grandchildren. Love it. Respect it. Preserve it. Protect it. Please.

I'll end this tirade with a verse from Don Willard's poem, Our Canyon*:

> The call of the canyon with its echoes shall bring
> Our hopes for renewal like flowers in the spring.
> And when the rocks and mountains shall fall,
> In no other place would my soul wait its call.

*(The full text of this poem can be found in Those Early Days, by the Sedona Westerners.)

Michael Coyote Peach
Sedona, Arizona
2013

Contents

"History would be an excellent thing if only it were true."
—   Leo Tolstoy

If You Die in Arizona, or, The Coffin Maker's Advice

Both of the incidents described in this poem are true. The first portion of this piece comes from an unpublished manuscript by the late Cecil Calvin Richardson, a former sheriff of Coconino County. The second part comes from a story by the late Roscoe G. Willson, "The Burial of the Cimarron Kid" from his book, No Place for Angels. Arizona Highways Magazine (April, 1991) published a photo which documents the Richardson story. I have engaged in some poetic license here. The name of the exhumed robber remains unknown, or at least questionable. Bob Thomas asserts in his article, "Shoot-Out in Canyon Diablo" (Arizona Highways, September, 1999) that the men who dug up the dead man insisted that pictures be taken so there would be a chance for someone to recognize and identify him. Bob Boze Bell, writing in True West Magazine (June, 2008), gives the dead outlaw's name as John Shaw, but goes on to say that even though pictures were taken, no one ever came forward to identify the dead man. Given this ambiguity, I've chosen to leave him nameless.

"If You Die in Arizona"
(The Coffin Maker's Advice)

A man may work from sun to sun, and woman's work is never done.
And there's no rest for the wicked 'til the grave.
But if you die in Arizona, (just in case nobody warned ya),
Those just might not be the rules by which the game is played.

So when shoppin' for a coffin, best look well and best look often.
And best make sure that its hinges are spry.
'Cause even when we've put you down, you're not that deeply underground.
And we're not necessarily done saying goodbye.

Take that gunslingin' desperado who got shot up in Canyon Diablo,
And his friends lamented how death had come in a blink.
And now that they reflected on it, it seemed plumb unfair, doggone it,
That they hadn't got to share one final drink.
And then one said, "Well, that's no trouble," and picking up a shovel,
They took a bottle up to old Boot Hill.
And in a flash they'd up and dug him, and with that bottle they did slug him.
Now that outlaw's ghost awaits his next refill.

So when shoppin' for a coffin, some are lush and some are Spartan.
But don't just settle for the one that costs the least.
'Cause even when you're six feet under, there are some who'll rend asunder,
And try to interrupt your well-deserved sleep.

Now, the Cimarron Kid just couldn't seem to simmer down,
And he got himself fired on a payday.
Oh, they stopped him short of branding the Chinese cook,
But it was his chicken ropin' that started the drunken melee.
In a Holbrook Saloon he continued his bender, and he got himself into a row
With a god-fearin', gun-totin', no nonsense bartender,
Who he shot through the shoulder – kapow!
But that barkeep shot back and put a bullet smack
In the space right between the Kid's eyes.
But if you think that that's the end, better think again, my friend…
The fun was only just beginning when he died!
So they put him a hearse and they gathered up a dearth of his friends,
And those attracted by the spectacle, and by the whiskey, of course.
And by that team of black horses, whose eyes seemed distorted,
And whose nostrils contorted, as they whinnied and snorted
And nervously cavorted in a way that seemed flat disrespectable.

Some dandy called Jersey, in lieu of the clergy, held the reins in one limp hand,
And stood up high on the seat, waved a bottle
And bleated out a toast to the departed man.
But the wind took his hat, and it flew like a bat
In between the lead horses in harness.
They bolted in terror, Jersey flew through the air,
And the ground tested out his head's hardness.
Off raced the hearse, and with a cheer and a curse
The cowboys gave spur to their mounts.
And to add to their fun, they discharged their six-guns.
That's a great horse motivator, it turns out.

Jersey sat up with a jolt, and gasping and choking
He asked what the heck had transpired.
And he didn't realize he'd just made himself the prize
Of a gaggle of quick-thinking liars.

"Why, it's the Kid! He's come back to life!
And now you'd better save your hide,
'Cause he didn't think much of your toast!"
And they giggled and hacked, and slapped each others' backs.
They relished their role in the hoax.
"Oh! So that's why they're a-shootin!" Jersey said.
"Well now, I'm rootin' fer them to put him under fer good!
After all, it's his funeral, and it'll surely ruin all
If he doesn't stay dead like he should!"

But that hearse's wild ride did finally collide
With the bank of a nearby arroyo.
And the choking dust settled, and the cowboys were nettled
At their fun's untimely end, boyo-boyo!
But the coffin had been ejected, and the Kid's corpse was detected
In the prickly embrace of a cactus.
So the cowboys pulled their ropes, and with a whole new spate of jokes,
They gave their riatas some practice.
And the lassoed remains were then tenuously retained
In the splintered remnants of the pine box.
And they stuck that underground, and then added plenty pounds
Of particularly heavy and fine rocks.
Then to pay their last respects as decorum directs,
They let fly with one last skyward volley.
This of course woke up Jersey, who, bedraggled and thirsty,
Uttered his ultimate folly:
"Gosh-almighty, boys, that's a most unwholesome noise
To mix with the pain in my head!
And I don't mean to seem hateful, but I'd really be most grateful,
If you'll promise you made sure he's truly dead!"

So when shoppin' for a coffin, don't let your standards soften.
Remember, you only get what you pay for.
It's for eternity you retire, but if in Arizona you expire,
Well, you never really know how long you'll stay for!

Kissin' Jenny

This piece is a prime example of that old saying, "never let the facts get in the way of a good story," (from which this book derives its title). The story has been written about by a number of respected Arizona historians including Frank Cullen Brophy, Budge Ruffner, and Arizona's official state historian, Marshall Trimble, but I have been unable to find any factual sources to back it up. Jay Field's <u>Arizona 1863-1912, A Political History</u>, while listing the names of all of the legislators in the 15th Territorial Legislature of 1889, makes no mention of anyone with a glass eye. Given its status as a "historical yarn," I felt free to embellish all aspects of this narrative, including the motives and behavior of the legislators, as well as Jenny's attributes and proclivities. If the story really is true, it is certainly in keeping with the spirit of much of the state's history.

Kissin' Jenny

Authority rests with the peoples' will.
Beauty lies in the eye of the beholder.
But power is seductive and if looks could kill,
Jealous glances would always grow bolder.
So it was that folks in Phoenix came to cast their eyes
On the prize of being the capital city.
And when the government assembled for the fifteenth time,
They got down to the nitty-gritty.

And in that Legislature, the southern counties showed their nature,
With smiles and with money changing hands.
But their fangs were quickly bared and no insult was spared
If the northern counties dared defy their plans.
Their invective was quite blistery as they cited the wandering history
From Fort Whipple to Prescott, and Prescott to Tucson, and back.
And now Prescott had better learn that Phoenix expected its turn.
So the southerners redoubled their attack.

The northerners spoke with grace of the Prescott capital's place
As more central within the boundaries of the Territory.
And they made a strong connection with the scenery's perfection,
And with early days of old Rough Rider glory.
But the southerners weren't moved and they strongly disapproved,
And they swore that they would bring it to a vote.
And the northerners surmised that the Phoenicians had paid bribes,
So the outcome looked to be extremely close.

This issue now was at its prime, so now if ever was the time
For all good men to come to the aid of their counties.
For the southerners matched an eye for an eye
With the loyal sons of Yavapai,
And all allies were poised to collect their bounties.
The northerners calculated, and they anticipated
That they might have only a one vote margin of victory.
But things could work out fine if they could hold the party line,
And if no one cast a vote that was contradictory.

But of all the faults to which men are heir, the one in which we all compare,
Is that morbid self-absorption known as vanity.
For when all is said and done, the truth is every mother's son
Is mantled with that aspect of humanity.
Now, among the blandishments of one of these northern gents,
Was the only glass eye in the whole Arizona Territory.
And as far as he was concerned, by possessing it he earned
Entitlement to a lion's share of glory.
His pride was plain to see to all in the gallery
When he'd rise to present a new bill in the chamber.
But he could turn a wrathful eye, whenever a vote was nigh,
On any who might favor a disclaimer.
And many such a politician had abandoned his convictions
And turned his criticisms into praise.
They would stammer and demure, rather than endure
The potent power of his porcelain gaze.

But the proof of his superiority (that was envied by the majority),
Was she on whom he lavished his affections.
A lady of the night, possessed of beauty bright,
And amply endowed with bounteous confections.
A courtesan without peer – one look and it was clear,
When it came to rivals that she hadn't any.
She could coo and she could sigh. She was the apple of his eye.
A buxom boudoir beauty known as "Kissin' Jennie."

Kissin' Jenny was a lusty gal, with adventurous appetites.
And it was said her featherbed was a garden of delights.
With her charms she caught his eye, with her talents she amused him.
And anything he cared to try, she never would refuse him.
And thus they whiled the nights away, carousing and love making.
She made him feel that all the world was his there for the taking.
And on her bedside nightstand, a glass of water was kept,
In which her guy would soak his eye, to clean it while he slept.

As that crucial vote grew near, the southern senators engineered
A tactic that was known to work on many.
For love turned cold can do one harm,
But the glow of gold can keep one warm.
And this fact wasn't lost on Kissin' Jennie.
For 'though she really loved her man, a girl's got to get it while she can,
And so she turned a blind eye toward her feelings.
Politics weren't her concern, she just seized an opportunity to earn.
She was already used to shady dealings.

So one night as her lover slept, secure in his renown,
Jennie took that glass in hand, and drank the contents down.
And as that orb slipped down her throat, southern victory was achieved.
It would be some hours after the vote before that eye could be retrieved.
The southerners knew her man was vain, and he would not show his face.
Nor would he cast a cyclopean vote, with just one eye in place.
His colleagues came to beg and plead, but their efforts came up hollow.

There in Prescott's hour of need, his pride he would not swallow.
Instead of conquering his vanity, he cowered like a rabbit.
And the chairman brought the gavel down, pronouncing, "The ayes have it."

In the aftermath of this decision, some called it a disgrace.
And some refused to accept the truth that stared them in the face.
Some could not believe their eyes, and accused the south of thieving.
But every politician knows that looks can be deceiving.
They'd thought the gleam in Jenny's eye meant love that would not fail.
But they should not have been surprised that her allegiance was for sale.

Kissin' Jennie was a thirsty gal, and she kept an eye on her future.
And when she found herself in the eye of that storm,
She did what she had to do, sir.
Women didn't have the right to vote, but Jennie didn't cry.
She seized that power by the throat
And changed things in the blink of an eye.

So the capital was moved to Phoenix, where it has since resided.
Through chicanery and lust and greed its location was decided.
And it may seem that corruption won, but at least we've learned one thing:
The poets are right. In the land of the blind, the one-eyed man is king.

Keep a Close Watch on Your Heart

In his book, <u>They Came To Jerome</u>, author Herbert V. Young tells an anecdote relayed to him by a distant relative of mine, Alfred Peach, Jr.. While employed in the Jerome mines, Alfred Jr. told Mr. Young about a fight he witnessed between two "hostesses" from the Fashion Saloon that took place around 1900. It was reported that the citizens may have actually disarmed the women before allowing the altercation to proceed, and that the spectators finally stopped the fight, declaring it a draw after both women had exhausted themselves. Given that Alfred was relaying an anecdote to begin with, I feel no qualms about making a slight dramatic embellishment in allowing the women to remain armed, and having their fight interrupted by the citizen's news. The rest of the particulars relating to the raffled watch, the young man and the two women, and his disappearance from Jerome, are true to Alfred's story.

Keep a Close Watch on Your Heart

In the wild, wild West it was considered best
To provide for one's own defense.
Evening the score was a necessary chore
Whenever things got too intense.
Many a slight could result in a fight
With fists or knives or guns.
Disputes were often settled with blood and metal
When all was said and done.
And volatile confrontations were not
The exclusive domain of men.

For Jerome was known to be the home of some fierce ladies of sin.
A local swain played a dangerous game, juggling the affections of two.
Knowing that if they found him out, could be the last thing he'd ever do.

One day a raffle was announced, a gold pocket watch as the prize.
And our Romeo was eager to be the light of his lovers' eyes.
So he vowed that he would win that watch, and then he swore an oath –
Separately he promised he'd bestow it on them both.
On the morning of the drawing, the fates made the swain their pawn,
As they engineered events to see that his was the name that was drawn.

And when those ladies heard his name called, they both shouted loudly,
Proclaiming their intentions to wear that timepiece proudly.
But when it was revealed each had an undetected rival,
That situation became one of questionable survival.

Now this Romeo wasn't the sharpest blade that ever carved a heart.
But he knew that pledging one watch to two girls had not been very smart.
For when they each became aware there was another claimant,
They both declared that they would dare to draw some blood as payment!
And in less than a harlot's heartbeat, their knives caught the morning light.
And the crowd cleared a cheering circle to make room for their catfight.
Hair was pulled, skin was scratched, and someone's blade caught flesh.
And just how far things might have gone was anybody's guess.

As the curses flew, and clothing tore, and the danger escalated,
A citizen pushed his way through the crowd, and hyperventilated.
The startled combatants broke apart. They'd lost their concentration,
As the breathless intruder panted the words that stopped their conflagration:
"Put up your knives, you fractious femmes! Your fighting now is fruitless.
Your cowardly boyfriend's fled Jerome! His promises are bootless."
The bloodied women stood agape. Their dresses hung in rags.
As faithless Romeo made his escape…with that watch in his saddlebags.

Now let me offer this advice, which you may not choose to heed.
But maybe these words will strike a note when you're in your hour of need.
The pretty face and gentle hands that catch one's eye when beckoning
May not prove worth a second glance when comes the hour of reckoning.
Emotions can turn fickle, and time will surely pass.
The sands are always trickling out of passion's hour glass.
Beauty may prove fleeting, and the mind begins to doubt
What has passed and what remains when time at last runs out.
So keep a close watch on your heart, and those you're keeping time with.
Beware the words of a silver tongue, no matter what they rhyme with.
It's easy to attract affections when one is in one's prime.
But only a faithful and loyal heart can stand the test of time.

The Story of Little Foot Fritz

The gist of this story is told by Ramos Sapello of the Western Writers of America in <u>Legends and Tales of the Old West</u> (1962). Mr. Sapello does not specify a location for these events, and given the book's title, we may assume the story is probably fictitious.

The Story of Little Foot Fritz

Time takes its toll on the body and soul of a cowboy out on the range.
There's searing sun, dust by the ton, endless chores, boredom, and mange.
There's rustlers and blisters, and prairie-rippin' twisters,
And occasional stampedes,
Grueling hours, infrequent showers, hard biscuits, bad coffee, and beans.
Cactus thorns, clothing torn, joints full of aches and pains.
And you sleep on the ground surrounded by the sound
And aroma of bovine methane.
There's freezing cold, and socks that mold,
There's scorpions, chiggers and fleas.
So it's no surprise one might fantasize about living a life of ease.
But of all the dreams and wild-eyed schemes to boldly strike it rich,
You'd have to give a hand to the cunning plan
Of that cowboy called Little Foot Fritz.

Little Foot was clever, Little Foot was wise.
Little Foot had hopes and dreams that no one else surmised.
Little Foot was clever, and Little Foot was intelligent.
And Little Foot planned for a future in which cows would be irrelevant.

So when the boys blew into town to let off steam and gamble,
Little Foot stayed separate, and by himself would ramble.
And while some of those 'pokes were sobering up,
Or recovering from their pranks,
Little Foot gazed demurely through the windows of the local bank.

Little Foot was clever, Little Foot was observant.
And he recognized a path he knew could lead to his preferment.
He saw an opportunity. He knew he'd have the means.
He made a careful study of bankers' hours and guards' routines.
Little Foot was clever, and Little Foot was insightful.
The bank would provide for a better life by filling his cash bags quite full.
And if he timed the business right, he wouldn't even have to shoot.
So the only remaining problem was where to hide the loot.
For a bunkhouse is a crowded place, devoid of privacy.
And Little Foot needed a secret space for the profit from his piracy.

And then one day he knew he'd come within reach of his goal,
When his pony plunged an errant hoof
Several inches down a prairie dog hole.
Little Foot stuck in his hand, removing fistfuls of earth,
And scooped out a space of sufficient shape
To hold a fat gold sack's girth.

Little Foot was clever, and Little Foot felt deserving.
So he steeled himself to do the deed that most would find unnerving.
And on that chosen day he felt confident and ready.
He had an alibi in place, and his nerves were steady.
He didn't really feel remorse. He wasn't committing murder.
And to throw suspicion off his track, he dressed like a hated sheepherder.
And with one final irony his disguise was made complete
When he pulled on a pair of oversized boots to hide his tiny feet.

It all went off without a hitch; his trail had not been found.
And he stashed the cash in his hidey-hole over in the prairie dog town.
Little Foot was clever. Little Foot was smart.
He even joined the posse, pretending to do his part.
Little Foot was clever, and Little Foot was patient.
He bided his time after the crime, 'til the Sheriff became complacent.
And when he was sure that no one watched, and everyone was sleeping,
He rode back down to the prairie dog town,
To fetch what he'd been keeping.

And he dreamed of the new life he would lead,
Being one hundred percent richer.
In a comfortable house on top of a hill,
Sipping whiskey from a golden pitcher.
In tailored suits with a silk cravat, and a cee-gar clenched in his jaw,
And diamond rings on his fingers – well beyond the reach of the law.

Yes, Little Foot was clever, and he'd made no mistake.
Now he'd leave this cowboy life behind to have and eat his cake.
But when he reached down to claim the prize
For which he'd schemed and planned,
An electric jolt shot up his arm, and the bag flew out of his hand!
And as the darkness gathered in, and his body convulsed in pains,
He crawled in the direction of his ill-gotten gains.
Next morning the boys at the bunkhouse were surprised to find his horse
Saddled, but without its master, so they backtracked its course.
And when they found Fritz' body, they gave a collective gasp
To see that swelling sack of gold…just inches from his grasp.

As to Little Foot Fritz' guilt there could be little doubt.
And it didn't take those cowboys long to get it figured out.
In that very secret space the bank robber had dug,
A digesting rattlesnake had coiled itself up snug.
And when Fritz' fingers groped for the bag, that snake had woke up mad.
So in spite of all his planning, the episode turned out bad.
For at that range, that snake just couldn't miss,
As attested by the twin holes in Little Foot Fritz' wrist.

Yes Little Foot was clever, an outlaw *bon vivant.*
But he hadn't figured that prairie dog hole
For a rattlesnake restaurant.
Little Foot was clever, and Little Foot was brave.
But the path of his desires only led to an early grave.

So in his quest for goals or gold a man may lie to his friends,
And work out ways to fool the law, and tie up all loose ends.
And he may mask illicit tasks and even face down danger.
But in spite of his brain, and his place in the food chain…
There's no escaping nature.

Photo by Jeff Wyckoff

The Legend of Old Brind

The late Dr. M.O. Dumas tells this allegedly true story in <u>Those Early Days</u>, which was published by the Sedona Westerners in 1968, and brought back into print in 2010 by the Sedona Historical Society. Some people claim the bull was known as "Brin" rather than "Brind." One of his most distinguishing features was said to be his brindled coat. Dumas uses the Brind spelling, but the current map and trail names are printed on USFS signs as Brins Mesa, omitting the possessive apostrophe. Dumas and others have referred to Brind as a bull, and it's doubtful that such an imposing animal would have been castrated, but it is sometimes necessary for me to preserve the rhyme scheme by referring to him as a steer. Dumas credits his legendary status to the fact that he managed to remain uncaptured for five or six years.

The Legend of Ol' Brind

Come listen, my children, and you will hear

Of the outright murder of a noble steer.

It was back in the days when you worked to survive,

And hardly a cowhand is still alive

Who remembers that famous freedom-loving steer,

Whose capture was a prize every cowboy held dear.

Old Brind was a Texan of the long-horned kind,

Gone wild for so long he could not be confined.

And all the Verde cowpokes longed for the glory they'd win

If they'd be the one to finally bring him in.

He ranged on that mesa southeast of Dry Creek.

Tough country for cowpokes, and no place for the meek.

Many had tried him, but to their chagrin,

That bull was triumphant, again and again.

One morning Ed Dickinson and Jimmie Van Deren

Spotted Old Brind at the edge of a clearing.

And feelin' their oats, they lit out with abandon.

And darn all the luck if their ropes didn't land on!

But before they could pull that wise bull to the ground,

He'd spotted a thicket, and headed them down.

Jimmie and Ed knew that those trees would sure kill them,

But they didn't look forward to the shame that would fill them

If they lost their ropes, and their friends should get wind of it...

They reckoned they never would hear the end of it.

For a cowboy who loses his rope is a greenhorn tenderfoot,

Subject to everyone's scorn.

So pulling their guns they shot old Brindle down,

And they coiled up their ropes and rode back into town.

Confessing the deed would have brought them dishonor,

So they never let on that that steer was a goner.

Cowpunchin' with their friends, can't you just imagine the tension?

Jim and Ed "shot the bull" whenever Brin's name got mentioned.

They kept it a secret, a memory hushed.

But when the carcass was discovered, they were seen to blush.

And finally the truth all came out in the wash.

And Jimmie and Ed were both kidded and joshed.

Those cow-killing cowboys never captured Ol' Brin.

And neither of them's

    got a mesa

      named after him.

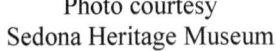

Photo courtesy
Sedona Heritage Museum

One Time in Ten

This poem is based on a story told by Albert Thompson in <u>Those Early Days</u> under the title "They Were Afraid of Each Other." The cattle economy was the first real industry established by the early Anglo settlers of the Verde Valley. Written accounts tell of longhorn steers "turning wild" after a season or more spent on the valley's open ranges, to the extent that if a cowboy could manage to get a rope on one, it would require careful work with a well-trained horse to get it tied to a stout tree. After two or three days in this condition, thirst would weaken the animal sufficiently that it could be brought in. Thus the custom of allowing "long-eared" calves to be taken on the open range was seen as a genuine boon to cowboys who otherwise had few prospects other than the wages ranchers might offer them for seasonal work. After much of the valley became part of the Coconino National Forest in 1905, the fencing of the various grazing allotments and the formation of various cattlemen's associations pretty much brought an end to the freedom of the open range and the chances of a lone cowboy starting up his own herd by acquiring unbranded yearlings without resorting to rustling. The behavior of both "Doc" Dumas and Joe Lay in this episode shows that despite their good reputations, and even though this practice was accepted as a custom among the valley's cattlemen, it was at best something of a gray area if the claim of ownership was challenged. The popular distain for rustlers and the value men placed on their own personal reputations was enough to keep many men from taking chances under questionable circumstances. Cattle and horse rustling may have been the origin of the term "moonlighting" as these unsavory practices were most often conducted after honest men's labors ended with the light of day.

One Time in Ten

In days gone by a man's wealth was tied to the size of his herd of cattle.

But a longhorn steer was hard to get near

And could put up one heck of a battle.

So some men found it easier to engage in dangerous behaviors.

Such unscrupulous types kept a running iron

For changing the brands of their neighbors.

But most good folks didn't have what it took

To live with a guilty conscience.

Because trust was sacred and a special kind of hatred

Was reserved for those involved in such nonsense.

And the punishment inflicted if caught and convicted

Was something to be feared.

So enterprising chaps kept their eyes out for calves

That were weaned but still long-eared.

A long-eared calf was a yearling that no longer ran with its mother.

And it could be yours if you gave it your brand before it bore any other.

An unbranded calf on the open range was one any cowboy could own.

But if you found it near land that a known outfit ran,

It was best just to leave it alone.

Most ranchers protected their cattle,

And could put a six-gun to good use.

And anyone suspected of rustling

Might wind up on the end of a noose.

But the custom of claiming these doggies

Allowed a cowboy to start his own herd.

So it was permitted and even admitted

If a man was as good as his word.

Still any long-ear's mother

Must reside on someone's ranch.

Earl Van Deren branding, 1949
Photo courtesy
Sedona Heritage Museum

So even in the best of circumstances, a cowboy was taking a chance.

Interpretation was bound to be subjective when claiming a calf was a stray.

So each cowboy had to decide for himself

Just how fast and loose he would play.

"Doc" M.O. Dumas and his friend Joe Lay were well-respected men.

They were known to do the right thing at least nine times out of ten.

They always pulled their own weight and stood on their own two feet.

And they never shied away from the work that it took to make ends meet.

One day these two companions were ridin' across the valley,

When Dumas allowed as he'd rest his horse, but Joe didn't want to dally.

So they said, "adios" and "hasta la vista" and Joe went on his way,
While Dumas stretched out there in the grass to watch the ravens play.
After a while, when his horse was refreshed, he climbed back in the saddle.
And he hadn't ridden long when he heard the distant sound of cattle.
When over a nearby ridge top came a sight that made him laugh.
Down that ravine came a healthy, gamboling, frisky long-eared calf!

Now Dumas was a practical man, aware of economy and thrift.
And he was grateful for the opportunity to receive such a timely gift.
So making sure that no one else was in that calf's vicinity,
He prepared for horse and rope and calf to unite in a buckaroo trinity.
But as he closed the distance, lasso circling overhead,
A movement on the other side of the draw filled him with sudden dread.
He'd been so intent on that little calf that he hadn't realized
That there was another horseman bearing down upon his prize!
So, assuming that calf's mother was a member of this other man's herd,
Dumas broke off his illicit pursuit, and fled without a word.
The route that he took homeward gave that area a wide berth.
The price that he'd almost had to pay for that calf
Was more than it would have been worth!
And as he rode he reflected on the lesson this experience had taught.
If mistaken for a rustler, he might easily have been shot!

Another day or two went by before Dumas saw Joe Lay,
And shared with him the details of what happened on that day.
But when he heard the story, Joe began to grin,
And asked his pal to repeat the part about how scared he'd been.
In the face of Joe's amusement, Dumas' anger began to rise.
At the very least he'd expected that his friend would sympathize.
"A lucky thing I wasn't killed, if this is how you'd behave.
You'd probably stand there laughing while they put me in my grave!
Just think of all the time gone by we've called each other friends,
But if that's all my life means to you, this where that friendship ends!"

"I understand," said Joe. "I know exactly how you feel.

But your life was never in danger even though it was a busted deal."

Joe could no longer contain his mirth, and he began to laugh.

"That was me you saw that day!

We spooked each other from that same little calf!"

Fear and guilt can trick one's sight, and play on one's credulity.

And a measure of risk goes hand in hand with any sudden opportunity.

So when it comes to your friends my lads, don't be too quick to judge them.

And if they laugh at your mistakes, that's nothing to begrudge them.

Those to whom you're closest, and in whom your trust is put,

Will likely do the same as you when the shoe's on the other foot.

And any time you're tempted to light out on a spree,

Remember there's a price to pay, and lunch is never free.

Don't be seduced by pie in the sky.

Keep your focus on the here and now.

And even when you can steal the milk,

It's safer just to buy the cow.

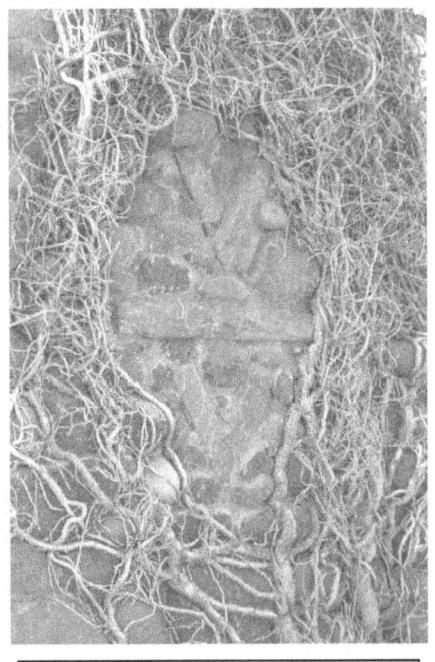

V Bar V brand on chimney,
V Bar V Ranch, Verde Valley

Ira and the Bad Cook

Earl Van Deren and Ira Smith
Photo courtesy
Sedona Heritage Museum

My source for this story was a published interview with the late Earl Van Deren, Ira Smith's brother-in-law (see "Little Bill"). Ira's daughter Mary Wyatt gave me several details about the story that caused me to make some additional changes to the rhyme scheme. I also added a few lines to clarify the fact that the stories the cowhands told about her father were made up in order to frighten the cook. The actual events revolved around the fact that the cook apparently didn't know how to prepare food any other way than by boiling it, thus instigating the cowboys' frustrations. When Ira entered the camp (having announced his arrival by firing his gun into the air), the cook fled on foot, and some of the cowboys, fearing for his safety in the wild country, trailed him. They said he was running so fast, his footprints were measured at more than four feet apart! They ultimately lost his trail and he was never heard from in these parts again. In spite of Earl's use of his brother-in-law's reputation for not tolerating poorly prepared food in this story, Ira Smith was known as a first rate cowhand, movie stunt man and horse wrangler, as well a popular dude ranch wrangler, which testifies to his true personality.

Ira and the Bad Cook

There's enough aggravation at roundup,
Without gettin' your insides all bound up.
But serving bad food can touch off a feud
If the cowboys complaints start to mound up.
On one particular drive, the cook's grub was sorely despised.
And his lack of care for the quality of his fare
Had the boys about fit to be tied.
They'd had their fill of his inedible swill,
And they were contemplating homicide.

The drive was now up on the Rim, but ever since way back in Bear Wallow,
This cook's culinary ineptitude had been more than the boys could swallow.
They'd choked down his gastronomic abuses,
And they were fed up with his half-baked excuses.
And the question they debated now was not so much the chow,
As which of them was best at tying nooses.

"His biscuits are as hard as rocks.
The coffee tastes like it's strained through old socks.
His beans will cause you grief – and what he does to the beef!
Why, that ought not to be done to an ox!"
"Boys, I am mightily vexed. This food shows a lack of respect
For the needs of a drover. And by the time this drive's over,
I expect we'll all be complete wrecks!"

"Cheer up, boys," said one of the hands. "I believe I just might have a plan
That will end our travail without landing us in jail
For having to put a bullet into that man.
Now things haven't been going so well,
And how much longer we'll last I can't tell,
But in a couple more days we'll be rounding up strays
With the boys from the good ol' X-L."

And those boys were sure glad to hear this.
Like they'd been pulled back from the edge of an abyss.
For among those X-L hands was a no nonsense man –
A tough hombre by the name of Ira Smith.
Now this managed to lighten their mood, and gave them a hopeful attitude.
For sure as lightning sparks a fire, the way to kindle Ira's ire,
Was to serve him up a plate of bad food.
"So before we merge our two herds, I say we drop a few well placed words
That'll singe our cook's ears when he overhears,
And we'll see if he'll take to his spurs!"

So over the next couple of days, the boys threw some phrases cook's way.
Words like, "incredibly strong," and, "won't stand it for long,"
And, "might bring his gun into play."
And when they saw they were spooking their quarry,
Those boys made up story after story.
Their lies and exaggerations caused the cook some vexation,
As well as considerable worry.

"I once saw him crop a cook's ears
When his steak was just a trifle over-seared.
When that burned meat was handed him,
The way he hogtied and branded him,
That cook might have been one of the steers!"
"When Ira said Cook used too much salt,
Cook said Ira's taste buds were at fault.
Ira whupped him so much that cook needed a crutch,
But it brought his over-salting ways to a halt!"
"One time our cook got too querulous
When Ira told him beans should be hairless.
Ira covered him with molasses and let the ants make a few passes
Just to teach him to not be so careless!"

Restored chuck wagon
on the Flying W Ranch,
Wichita, Kansas

"When Ira said cook's food was not delicious,
Cook told Ira to just mind his own business.
Ira smacked him so hard that cook fell in the lard.
Took him a week to get over his dizziness!"

Thus they scrambled the cook's wits and they fried his nerves,
And they made sure his emotions got thoroughly stirred.
Then to add to his anguish, they peppered their language
With a few more well-seasoned words.
Terms like "hot tempered, thoroughly dismembered, intolerant,"
And, "justifiably murdered".

So when Ira finally rode into camp, Cook's palms felt immediately damp.
For 'though the stories were fabricated, Cook was so agitated,
Ira more than lived up to their stamp.
The boys all hollered and cheered. And as the cook cowered and peered,
Ira glared about and left no doubt he was indeed a man to be feared.
His beard was like a grizzly bear's pelt. Cook's knees began to melt.
He wore huge bat-winged chaps, and Cook almost collapsed
When he saw the big .45 strapped to Ira's belt!
So frankly assessing his talents,
'Cause it didn't look like Ira'd make allowance,
Cook elected to fly (without saying goodbye).
He was sure his life hung in the balance!
He just silently slipped away, and he hasn't been seen to this day.
He just straddled his saddle and quickly skee-daddled,
Without even collecting his pay!

And the boys were pleased with their knavery,
And with the cook's manifest lack of bravery.
Because despite his tough looks, Ira was a heck of a good cook.
So for the rest of the drive,
The boys knew their meals would be more savory.

Oak Creek Roundup, 1921
Photo courtesy
Sedona Heritage Museum

Climax Jim

Some authors give this man's last name as Nephew, while others spell it Nephews. I have gone with the latter as this seems to be the majority opinion. A favorite of those who enjoy writing about Arizona's more outlandish characters, he can be found in <u>Rattlesnake Blues, Dispatches from a Snakebit Territory</u>, by Leo W. Banks, and in both <u>Tales of Arizona Territory</u> and <u>Arizona Trails and Tales</u>, by Charles D. Lauer. Arizona State Historian Marshall Trimble and Bob Boze Bell, editor of <u>True West Magazine</u>, have also told tales of "Climax Jim." Rufus Nephews, alias "Climax Jim" resided in Clifton, a rough-and-tumble mining town in eastern Arizona.

The "Hashknife" Outfit was the Aztec Land and Cattle Company, one of the earliest livestock and real estate corporations of the West, although it was organized and directed from New York City. The company ran approximately 60,000 head of cattle on a range including one million acres it purchased from the Atlantic and Pacific (later Santa Fe) Railroad for fifty cents an acre. The corporation's brand resembled the shape of a cook's knife and thus became their moniker. Perhaps due to its distant headquarters, the Hashknife Outfit is reputed to have employed many outlaws and killers who were on the run from crimes committed elsewhere, and who engaged in other instances of lawless activity while in northern Arizona, including rustling their employers' cattle. Ironically, when the Arizona Rangers were formed in 1901, Burt Mossman, the former Trail Boss of the Hashknife Outfit, was chosen as its first captain. Arizona Territorial Governor Nathan Oakes Murphy reasoned that, since Mossman had been able to clean up the unruly Hashknife Outfit, he'd be the right man to head up Arizona's first police force.

Climax Jim

A young man left his boyhood home in Washington, D.C.,
And lit out for the Wild West, a cowboy for to be.
He'd never lived the cowboy life. He didn't know much about it.
But he managed to wrangle himself a job
With the notorious Hashknife outfit.
He knew it was a handicap that he came from "back East."
And he knew if they thought he was a tenderfoot,
He soon might be deceased.
But creating a tough reputation was something he hadn't planned out.

So he'd have to latch on to something bold if he was going to stand out.
Those Hashknife boys were a swaggering bunch.
They could be downright whacko.
So he stuffed his mouth with copious amounts of Climax Chewing Tobacco.
The cowboys were impressed to see his cheeks full to the brim.
And that's how Rufus Nephews became known as "Climax Jim."

He quickly learned the ins and outs of working with those cows.
But when it came to honesty, he'd never taken vows.
He knew he'd never get anywhere, fighting an uphill battle,
If he spent all his working time punchin' other peoples' cattle.
So he learned to use the running iron that rustling demands.
And he became quite skillful at altering other's brands.
For rustling in Apache County, Rufus went on trial.
The attorney read the charges that the court was going to file.
Rufus produced witnesses he knew would not betray him.
They swore he had stolen the cattle…
But it was down in the county of Graham!
So Climax Jim was acquitted, but the charges were filed again.
This time Graham County would impanel twelve good men.
But again those trusty witnesses brought an end to the legal show time.
They swore it was in Apache County that Rufus had burgled those bovines.

Climax Jim, oh Climax Jim, there is no outlaw quite like him.
You can talk about Durango Dan or Amarillo Slim,
But if you ask the folks in Clifton, there's no one like Climax Jim.

Now Climax wasn't clever, not crafty like a fox.
So as a matter of necessity, he got good at picking locks.
And soon whenever a crime occurred, and there was no sign of a break in,
They just assumed that Climax Jim had picked the lock and done the takin'.
Frequently they caught him, and they threw him in jail again.
But it wasn't a question of would he escape. It was only a matter of when.
Finally, at the prison in Yuma, he served a full year's sentence.
But his willingness to submit that time was not about repentance.
He said he was only interested in his neck retaining its shape.
'Cause he didn't care for the way it would stretch,
If they caught him tryin' to escape.

Climax Jim, oh Climax Jim, no jail in Arizona could hold the likes of him.
You can talk about Montana Mike or Tularosa Tim,
But if you ask the folks in Clifton, there's no one like Climax Jim.

Another time ol' Climax was brought before the court.
For cashing stolen payroll checks the law brought him up short.
The prosecutor laid the evidence on the table in front of the defendant,
And Rufus saw that his chances had just become ascendant.
He whispered to his lawyer, who then leaped to his feet,
And called the prosecutor a liar and a cheat!
Those in the court were startled by the force of this objection.
And Rufus waited until all eyes were turned in the lawyers' direction.
He deftly placed his tobacco pouch upon that damning check,
Then pulled them both back to his lap so no one could detect.
Those gesticulating lawyers held the jury's rapt attention.
And Rufus calmly used them as his unwitting henchmen.
He wadded up the evidence together with some leaf,
Then sat back to watch the fracas as he tucked them in his cheek.
He spat out the tobacco, and confidently chewed,
Quietly enjoying the circus of the court's ineptitude.
At last the judge's gavel brought an end to the confrontation,
And the prosecuting attorney prepared for his summation.
He recapped all his arguments in his most dramatic voice.
"The defendant has taken the outlaw trail, and that has been his choice.
But he can not evade the law, nor its investigation.
And now he'll have to feel the wrath of society's indignation.
We have produced the evidence," (here his voice rose to a shout)
"And it shall prove him guilty, of that there is no doubt!"
But as he strode to the table, to show the court the check,
All he saw was Rufus, calmly scratching his neck.
His habit of chewing tobacco proved to be his best defense
As he regained his freedom by swallowing the evidence!

Climax Jim, oh Climax Jim, his fingers were light, but his mind was dim.
An outlaw diamond in the rough, he was a crusty gem.
And if you ask the folks in Clifton, there's no one like Climax Jim.

They caught him stealing horses outside of Springerville.
But when they brought him to the jail, the sheriff's voice was shrill:
"He's had no time for hygiene, out on the outlaw path.
So before you put him in my jail, he's got to have a bath!"
And indeed his body odor was enough to make them cough,
So they all held their noses and pointed to the horses' trough.
Then they retired to the saloon, leaving Rufus to his ablutions.
They firmly hoped a good, long soak would lessen his pollutions.
But as he stepped into the water, Rufus saw a fine-looking horse.
And abandoning the soap and brush, he acted without remorse.
He left his clothing where it lay, and jumped on the horse's back.
And in an act of naked villainy, he set off down the track.
He paraded down Springerville's main street, like the famous Lady Godiva.
Women stared in disbelief, men ejected their saliva!
This same trail served Eager as that town's main thoroughfare.
And Mormon eyes saw Rufus bounce by, without any underwear!
The citizens were surprised and stunned, their faces shocked and reddened,
As Rufus' ride in his birthday suit became the stuff of legend.

The Southwest has its characters, its heroes and its refuse.
But few attained the stature of that outlaw Rufus Nephews.
Some outlaws went for liquor and guns when they were in a bad mood,
But Climax Jim had the confidence to commit crimes in the nude.
He didn't rely on an alibi. There was nothing he was hiding.
And he clearly gave new meaning to what's known as bareback riding.

Climax Jim, oh Climax Jim, he wasn't polite and he wasn't prim.
But he was full of vigor, and he was full of vim.
And if you ask the folks in Clifton, there's no one like Climax Jim.

A Verde Valley Cowboy Speaks His Mind About a New, So-Called "Game"

This piece is certainly more of a rant than a poem, and is meant to convey the attitude of local cowboys – to whom baseball, hunting, horseshoes, wrasslin', and rodeo were the only legitimate "sports" – toward the intrusion of this foreign-born diversion into their domain. The part about the two advocates being tarred and feathered is alleged to be true. Herbert V. Young tells of the game's gradual acceptance and development in the Verde Valley in his book, They Came to Jerome.

A Verde Valley Cowboy Speaks His Mind About a New, So-Called "Game"

"How in the devil's name did a thing like this get started? I'm talkin' about this namby-pamby, piss ant, pipsqueak, sissy boy waste of time called "golf"! What kind of a name is that, anyway? And have you seen those pants they wear? "Plus Fours", they're called. They look like a cross between a really bad pair of trousers and a set of chaps, but they don't successfully make neither. Now you may find me holdin' a branding iron or a pistol, an' I'll go to my grave with my lariat in my hand, but you wouldn't catch me dead holdin' some strange shaped piece of hickory called a "mashie", a "brassie", or a "niblick". I cain't hardly say those things without laughin'. They call this a game? 'Bout the same as snipe huntin' if you ask me. Now some of the hoity-toity set in Jerome have taken it up, but I expect they'll recognize ain't nothin' manly in it sooner or later. An' I seen two cowpokes tarred and feathered for calling it a sport in the presence of some of the players on the Jerome baseball team! I predict it'll die off. It'll never have much future in this valley. One thing's certain – no one's ever gonna make an honest living from it."

Isadore Christopher

This story is alleged to be true. If so, it doesn't speak highly of military powers of observation. On the other hand, soldiers of that era saw many unfortunate victims of Apache torture, so perhaps it is plausible that a skinned bear carcass could be taken to be the burned corpse of a human being. Christopher ran his cattle under the C I brand in the Pleasant Valley area during the time of the range war between the Graham and Tewksbury factions, but he does not seem to have taken an active part in the hostilities. Another detail about Mr. Christopher is that he would add the hair from his hogs to the mortar in between the logs of his cabin.

Isadore Christopher

Isadore Christopher was a hairy man,
Who built a ranch on a creek that still bears his name.
By the Apaches he was hated, and repeatedly raided.
They delighted in putting his home to the flame.
One day our Mister Christopher killed himself a bear,
Nailed up its hide and hair, and then he went away.
The Apaches came around, and burned his place to the ground.
As they would have done on this, or any other day.
Soldiers came and chased them off, and there in the ashes –
Horrors! They thought they saw…
The scorched and stinking corpse of poor old Izzy!
And rendered thereby sorely sad, and maybe driven slightly mad,
They made decisions that could rightly be called "dizzy".
So they laid that body down in the dark and bloody ground,
And the funeral was marked by true despair.
So when Izzy returned from his hunting,
He didn't want to seem affronting,
So he waited a while before he told them they'd buried that bear!

Justice, Revenge and Memory: The Anatomy of a Killing

J.J. Thompson was the first white settler in Oak Creek Canyon, claiming a homestead there in 1876. Within a couple of years of his arrival, he had convinced his friend Abraham James to move his family from Nevada to the red rock country. The James' were the first homesteaders within what are now the city limits of Sedona, and Abraham is credited with naming many of the prominent buttes and rock formations of the surrounding area. Not long after the arrival of the James family, Jim Thompson married Margaret James, the sixteen-year-old daughter of Abraham and Elizabeth James. Thompson was twenty-four years older than his bride. They ultimately had nine children, the first of whom was Frank, the first white child born in Oak Creek Canyon. Jim Thompson partnered with Richard Wilson, a bear hunter who came into the area not long after Thompson. Wilson helped the Thompsons with their farming. In 1885, Jim Thompson was summoned to Prescott to give testimony in the trial of Charles Sterling, a rustler and counterfeiter who homesteaded at Sterling Springs, at the head of Oak Creek Canyon. (Thompson and other members of a posse that included William Munds and his son, Jim, caught Sterling and discovered his counterfeiting activities, then delivered him into the custody of Justice of the Peace John Goodwin at Jerome.) Wilson had recently come across the tracks of a huge grizzly bear, but his large caliber hunting gun was in need of some repair. He asked Thompson to take the gun to a gunsmith's in Prescott. In return for this favor, Wilson agreed to check in on Margaret, three-year-old Frank, and one-year-old Lizzie Thompson every evening during J.J.'s absence.

Part One: Maggie Thompson Prays

While the circumstances of this story are true, the words here are not Margaret Thompson's. I have endeavored to imagine what her thoughts and feelings might have been during this ordeal, and to convey the sense of vulnerability and anxiety that she might have felt during the eight days between her husband's departure and the discovery of Wilson's body. Wilson Mountain and Wilson Canyon were named for him in the aftermath of his killing.

Maggie Thompson Prays

I

"Oh, Jim...I'm so worried. Mr. Wilson told you he'd stop by every evening, but you've been gone four days and we haven't seen him yet. You did make him promise to leave that grizzly bear alone until you got back, didn't you? I try to keep occupied with the chores so my mind won't dwell on it, but it's hard. Last night I heard a mountain lion up on the cliffs. It sounded like a woman screaming. I'm afraid the cow or the pigs might attract that bear, or the Apaches. I wish my daddy was still alive. My mind would be easier if he could be here. Please hurry back."

Margaret Thompson
Photo courtesy
Sedona Heritage Museum

II

"Six days now you've been gone. I keep thinking that one day those Indians whose crops were here when you came will show up and demand their land back. You laugh and remind me it's been a few years since there were any Indians in this part of the country, and I doubt they would come up this way with the officers fishing down at Camp Garden...but I find I grow more nervous with each day you're gone. Every rustling shadow of the canyon becomes a beast, an Indian, or a raving madman. I pray I am not called upon to use the pistol you left. And I know it's not fair...but curse that Mister Sterling for making the court call you away from us."

III

"Thank God! Judge Goodwin and his son Tom arrived from Jerome. The first human beings we've seen in eight days! They wanted to use the cabin up the creek for some trout fishing. I told them Mr. Wilson had the only key and that I was desperately worried since he'd never appeared. The Judge said he must have gotten involved with things at the farm. But I said he would have kept his promise if it was humanly possible. So they agreed to ride up the canyon and look for him. When they came galloping back so soon...I knew the news would be bad. They'd found what was left of him, thanks to his dog staying with the body and barking. And the Judge sent Tom to bring back enough men to hold a coroner's inquest. But he said that, from what they'd found, it sure looked like that bear had got him. Until such time as Tom and the others return, the Judge has been so kind as to agree to remain here. Still I can't feel that little Frank and Lizzie are truly safe with that bear still out there somewhere. May justice be swift and may God watch over us all until we are together again."

Part Two: Richard Wilson's Killer Speaks

The story of Richard Wilson's death is one of the best known pieces of Oak Creek Canyon history, and the names Wilson Mountain and Wilson Canyon both commemorate it, but I have always found it interesting to imagine it from the bear's point of view. Several years after Wilson's death, George Thompson returned home carrying a huge bear skull, which he said he'd found with an enormous skeleton in the thick brush of Wilson Canyon. It is reported that George was alone when he made this discovery, but as I am already employing considerable literary license in this piece, I place him in company with a second child in order to articulate what may have been his thoughts.

Wilson's hunting knife was not found with the body, leading to speculation that he might have wounded the bear with it during their struggle. Jim Thompson asked George to return to the skeleton to see if he could find Wilson's missing hunting knife, thus proving this was the same bear, but George was never able to find the remains again. Many years later, an old, rusty knife blade was found in the mouth of Wilson Canyon, which is the approximate area where his encounter with the bear is believed to have taken place. This blade is in the possession of the Sedona Heritage Museum, but there has never been a conclusive determination that it is in fact the blade from Wilson's knife. Unless someone one day stumbles upon the skeleton of a grizzly bear with Wilson's knife embedded in one of its bones, we may never really know if Wilson actually killed the bear.

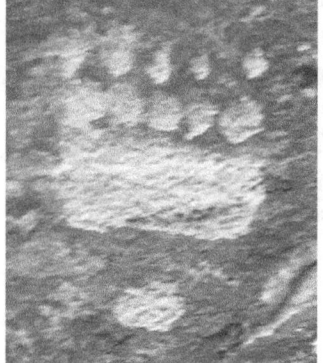

Petroglyph of a bear track,
Red Tank Draw, Verde Valley

Richard Wilson's Killer Speaks

This was my land, before you came.
And before me the land of my father, and his father,
And his father before him,
Back into the beginning of all things.
We ruled here with unquestioned authority, unchallenged mastery,
Unrivaled ferocity.

Only the great jaguar might give us pause.
We were worshipped by the ancient ones,
Who carved our tracks into the rocks, and saw in us
Great power to heal, and deep understanding.

And then you came,
And did what even lions had not dared to do before you:
To stand in our way, to question our right,
To put a bounty on our lives.

So when you found my track it was with anger,
And not with awe and respect, that you measured it.
And your mind began to fashion traps to usurp my sovereignty.
To you I was not owner, but invader.
And in all this I had done nothing to you personally.
The land is big and should have room enough for both of us.
But you say my needs cannot be in harmony with yours,
And we cannot exist in this world together.

So that evening when you came unexpectedly upon me,
Spooking the burros and scattering the new potatoes across the river rock,
You might have just moved on, and I'd have been happy with either –
The starchy strangeness of the tubers
Or the stringy flesh of your beasts of burden,
You might have reflected that your young dog was new
And unused to encounters with my kind.
And that you'd sent your big weapon for repair –
The weapon with which, in your mind, you had so many times
Imagined the circumstances of my death.
And now you had only your small gun.

I know I gave you warning of your trespass,
But your lack of respect for my territory, your lack of flight,
Was a challenge boiling in my blood.
With a roaring in my ears I repeated my warning and stepped toward you.

Yet even here I still might not have charged,
Had you but backed away softly, respectfully.
But when you stood and raised your weapon,
The rage of my ancestors thundered in my breast,
And hatred filled my lungs, my throat, my eyes.
You made yourself a threat too great to ignore.
Just then the fire flashed, and pain tore into me.
In shock and surprise I turned and ran, hoping you would not follow.
The howling of your dog told me that you did.

Instinct took over, and I knew I must save myself.
So I turned into the trees and waited,
The foolish dog failed to warn you as I'd hoped,
And I struck, claws tearing down head and body.
The weapon fell, screaming out its terrible fire again.
In my hesitation you tried climbing a tree,
But our struggle had progressed beyond the point
Where more than one of us could leave it alive.
I caught your downward kick in my mouth,
And tore off your boot as you almost tore off that limb,
Screaming and cursing as I pulled you down to your fate.
But there it was again! – another searing pain, stabbing into me!
The stench of my own blood – horrible!
And again I ran, for the moment blinded by shock and shame,
Not even caring whether I'd finished you.
My fury was like a whirlwind as I realized
The force of life was draining from me.
I dragged myself up into the thick brush.
I, who never suffered defeat in a hundred trials,
Felt the cloying darkness closing in around me.
And the things I last remember were the pain, humiliation and disbelief…
And the awful barking of your damned dog!

And now I am awakened after a long, long sleep.
I do not feel hunger. I do not feel anything. I am naked.
Someone has stolen my beautiful coat and my powerful muscles.
I cannot lift my claws nor make a sound
As these noisy boys and their slobbering dogs –
Again these damned dogs, hounding me from my peace!
Stumble over me, through me, and stand now, gaping and panting,
Eyes wide in disbelief.

"What is it?"
"You mean, what was it?"
"Was it a dinosaur?"
"Nah. Looks like a bear."
"But it's so huge!"
"Griz, prob'ly. Been dead a long time."
"Let's take the skull home with us. No one'll believe us otherwise."

So once again I was violated.
My bones trampled, chewed, and removed,
To undergo another transformation,
From keepsake to curiosity, and to gather dust,
Fingers occasionally penetrating my vacant sockets,
Until I am at last abandoned to my fractured eternity.

This was my land, until you came.
But perhaps someday the fingers of new landlords
Will fondle your disinterred remains.
And you, lamenting your own forgotten glory, will understand.
Your power is just an echo carried on the wind.
And your mighty tracks are trampled underfoot by new interlopers
And their ill-mannered dogs.

Part Three: Jim Thompson Visits the Grave of His Friend

Jim Thompson returned from Prescott after Richard Wilson had been buried in newly-named Wilson Canyon. The words here are purely from my own imagination. Ever since I learned the story of Wilson's death, I have been intrigued by what Jim Thompson must have thought and felt about it. When he learned of his friend's death, Thompson's mind must have swirled in a vortex of interconnected events. Wilson built at least two of the cabins that the Thompson family lived in at Indian Gardens. Jim and his friend B.F. Copple had discovered the butchered calf whose trail had led the posse to Sterling. When the posse was returning from having arrested Charles Sterling and his partner, they stopped at Indian Gardens where Wilson had taken possession of the outlaws' weapons. The posse had turned Sterling over to Judge Goodwin who, along with his son Tom, would be the ones to discover Wilson's body while Thompson was away giving testimony at Sterling's trial. Wilson had been leading some burros laden with bags of new potatoes to feed to the Thompson's pigs. Perhaps that is what had attracted the bear's attention to him? Wilson didn't have his powerful rifle with him because he'd given it to Thompson to take to Prescott. I imagine a mixture of grief, anger, blame, and irony among Jim's thoughts as he bids goodbye to his friend and partner.

Some time later, Wilson's grave was exhumed and his remains were re-buried in the mouth of Munds Canyon, up above the Thompson homestead at Indian Gardens.

Jim Thompson Visits the Grave of His Friend

"Well, old hunter, looks like the tables finally turned. You broke your promise to me. Judge Goodwin said it looked like you'd come on that bear on the way down to my place. Prob'ly that very first night I was gone. Guess you just couldn't resist takin' a shot, even with your small rifle. Did you remember your dog was new and untrained when you trailed the blood into this box canyon? Too confident to believe you could be ambushed. That bear was only a couple feet away when it hit you. Knocked the gun from your hands. No choice but to run. They showed me your boot. The heel was nearly ripped off. I could fit my finger into a couple of the teeth marks. I saw the limb you almost pulled off that tree, tryin' to hold on as the bear dragged you down. They told me half your face was gone, but you still managed to get yourself to the water. Well, I'll give you this, Richard Wilson, you're a tough old Scotsman. That grizzly didn't kill you. The Coroner says you drowned, tryin' to drink from the creek."

Jim Thompson at Richard Wilson's gravesite
Photo courtesy
Sedona Heritage Museum

The Ghosts of Wilson Canyon

The following poem is a fantasy, based on the history discussed in the three previous pieces. To the best of my knowledge, no one has ever reported a supernatural encounter in the vicinity of the site where Richard Wilson is presumed to have encountered the bear.

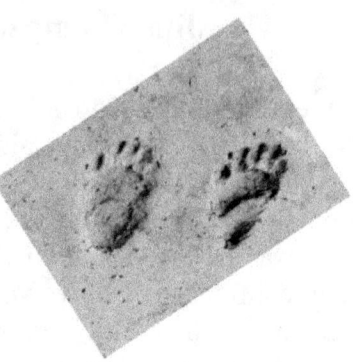

The Ghosts of Wilson Canyon

On a moonlit night if you take a walk over rocks in Oak Creek Canyon,
You may come to a place where the past is embraced
And a spirit will not be abandoned.
As the sycamores stand like sentinels and wave their arms in the wind,
The clatter of hooves on the stones is heard,
And a tragedy unfolds…again.
The braying of burros, the bark of a dog, and the growl of a startled bear.
Then the desperate sound of a rifle shot is carried on the air.
Then the panicked scatter of animals and the panting breath of a chase
Trail off to the west up a canyon to keep their appointment with fate.
Then the shadows shift and the only sound is the rustling of leaves.
And you laugh at yourself for believing in the tricks that the mind conceives.
And you take a deep breath and rationalize
That your nerves have been playing a joke.
And it's only your imagination…but isn't that the smell of gun smoke?
And now your hairs are bristling as another shot shatters the silence,
Followed by screams and snarling howls
And the sounds of horrible violence.

Then in an instant it's over, and silence reclaims the void.
And you struggle to maintain your composure,
And to stop being so paranoid.
You are the master of your will, the captain of your feelings.
These phantom terrors can not chill, nor set your senses reeling.

For creatures of lesser nature, the choice is fight or flight.
But man is the caretaker, and sees with wisdom's light.
It was only the wind in the branches, and the sound of the burbling water.
After all, more than a century's passed since that old man was slaughtered.
But the determination to keep his word
And the promise he made to his friend…
Could that penetrate through wrinkles in time, to echo here now and again?
Could the guilt of a task unfinished and a promise that wasn't fulfilled
Remain yet so undiminished in this place where the old man was killed?
Can such powerful psychic impressions manifest across the years?
Or are they only the suggestions of our over-active fears?
Between environment and imagination, it's easy to get carried away.
But this nervous hoax and old Wilson's ghost
Will vanish with the light of day.
By now you've managed to calm yourself with a firm grasp of reality,
And you'll give no further credence to these wisps of abnormality.
You've analyzed this fantasia as sprung from historical disaster.
Just a temporary aphasia that made your heart beat faster.
We make ourselves the victims in a superstitious season.
But the spell of wind and moonlight can't sustain in the light of reason.
Animals are slaves to instinct, but the human race
Has harnessed the power of intellect to put fear in its place.

Then your nostrils flare from the acrid smoke
That came from someone's gun.
And the sound of branches breaking sets your feet off at a run!
And a wave of terror envelops you and defeats your self control.
And your only thought is to do what you must to save your mortal soul.
And as you flee that cursed place your wits are quite agog.
But try as you will, you can't outpace
The mournful baying of the old man's dog.

The Hauntings of the "Red Ghost"

United States Secretary of War Jefferson Davis (later president of the Confederate States of America) had become convinced that camels would provide a superior means of transporting military supplies across the deserts of the southwest. It is interesting that Davis lighted on the idea of using camels. Camelids had originally evolved in ancient North America, but had been rendered extinct in their original homeland by the late Pleistocene. Fortunately, they had successfully migrated into Asia and Africa. At Davis' recommendation, Congress appropriated $30,000 to import seventy-five camels from Africa and Asia Minor. Both Dromedary and Bactrian camels were imported along with some North African camel drivers, the most famous of whom was Hadji Ali, whose name was Americanized as "Hi-Jolly." Hi-Jolly is memorialized in Quartzite, by a pyramid-shaped monument topped with a camel. In 1857, John B. Floyd, who had replaced Davis as Secretary of War, decided to put the camels to the test on a survey of the first wagon road across northern Arizona. Floyd put the expedition under the direction of Lieutenant Edward (Ned) F. Beale of the Army Topographical Engineers. Beale had been a naval officer and Indian agent. As an explorer, Beale had already crossed the continent three times and had surveyed a railroad route along the 38th parallel. Like Davis, Beale championed the idea of using camels for the expedition, as they could travel great distances without water, could feed off of whatever forage might be available, and could carry heavy loads in hot and dry conditions. Yet in spite of this nineteenth century homecoming, they were not warmly welcomed. Beale wrote a glowing report to Secretary Floyd in which he claimed that his soldiers had come to prefer the camels to the stubborn temperament of mules. Despite Beale's hyperbole, it is likely that the common soldiers objected to the camels' habits of spitting on them, to say nothing of their penchant for kicking and biting. Horses were panicked at the scent and sight of these humped and shaggy beasts. The eruption of hostilities at the outset of the Civil War brought the camel experiment to an end, and the army sold some of the camels to circuses, gave some to the Navajo people, and turned the rest loose into the desert. The Navajos apparently found their camels better for eating than for riding. For a brief period, some of the army camels were used to transport mail between Fort Tejon, near Los Angeles, and Albuquerque, New Mexico, but stage coaches and later railroads rendered this on obsolete practice. Even as the military's experiment with camels was ending, private enterprise was investigating the idea of using them. In 1863, Otto Esche imported fifteen Bactrian camels from Mongolia with the idea of using them to transport salt from California to the silver mines of Nevada's Comstock Load. This attempt also failed, again due to their negative reception by humans and horses. Nevada even passed a law that camels could only use city streets in the hours between midnight and dawn when most horses and mules would be resting in livery stables. Esche released his remaining camels into the Nevada desert, where it is presumed they died without reproducing. It has been claimed that the last of the wild camels in Arizona's deserts had perished by the early twentieth century, but a friend of mine who grew up in Quartzite told me he saw a family of wild camels in the desert near there in the early 1960s, and it was not uncommon during my boyhood in Phoenix to hear of hunters or jeep enthusiasts claiming to have encountered an occasional solitary camel in the shimmering heat of the Sonoran desert. Such sightings were mostly ascribed to alcohol or heat-induced hallucinations. I found and photographed an excellently rendered petroglyph of a camel in the red rock country of the Mogollon Rim near Sedona. I suspect this glyph was probably made by a Yavapai Indian who may have seen one of the original decommissioned army camels, or perhaps one of their elusive descendants. This poem is based on a true story told by Arizona State Historian Marshall Trimble in his book, Arizoniana, Stories from Old Arizona. Budge Ruffner reports a possible camel sighting west of Ajo in 1939 in his book, All Hell Needs is Water.

The Hauntings of the "Red Ghost"

A group of prospectors on the Verde River
Passed a night that would test their faith.
At the darkest hour their camp was attacked
By a cloven-footed, red-haired wraith.
And after the monster fled into the night, and the moon had risen to full,
They gazed in horror at what it left behind – a grinning human skull!

A number of victims would lose their lives,
Kicked and trampled beyond repair.
And always the surrounding bushes bore some strands of coarse red hair.
And thus the monster traveled, and thus the legend grew.
And with repeated sightings, it was proven to be true.
And with each new encounter, the details remained the same,
And gave rise to a mystery, shocking and insane.
Some called it the Muggy-Own Monster,
Indians whispered of the dreaded "Red Ghost".

And newspapers didn't scruple for facts
When besting their competitors' boasts.
"A Sign of the Apocalypse!" Headlines railed in boldest print.
And as far as the preachers were concerned, this demon was heaven-sent.
Accounts of alleged "witnesses" were great for news circulation,
And there's nothing quite like a monster for swelling your congregation.

But if the sight of the Red Ghost by itself
Weren't enough to bring on madness,
It bore a grizzly companion, a partner in its sadness.
To call it a hallucination brought on by being *muy borracho*,
Couldn't lessen the intimidation of this macabre *muchacho*.
From whatever fiery corner of heck this long-necked demon came,
On its back it bore the carcass of a rider from beyond the grave.
This fearsome apparition could turn one's knees to gelatin.
For strapped across the mountainous hump of its back,
Was a flailing, headless, human skeleton!

Then came the day a rancher took its life with his Winchester.
And when it came to explaining the Red Ghost's "hauntings"
There was many an artful jester.
'Twas deduced that it must have been a remnant
Of the military's Araby experiment
That was interrupted by the Civil War.
But Jeff Davis' bold vision had been treated with derision.
And this one escaped, or got turned out wild,
And somehow managed to survive.
'Though those rawhide straps had rubbed its body sore.

All agreed that this hideous specter
Was the worst ever sucked Nature's nectar.
And 'twas feared that they might be attacked again
By another such ghost-ridden Bactrian.
But was it just a little more scary,
Because those bones sat astride a dromedary?

But who had tied the rider on?
What malevolent marauder had condemned this beast to its career
Of terrifying slaughter?
And had that wretched jockey perhaps still been alive
When roped atop his hell-bound hearse?
What horror to contrive!
What fault deserved the strictness of this sentence?
What sin merits penance so egregious?
To be baked by the merciless sunlight;
Torn by vultures like a mobile Prometheus?
Was it primitive justice, or punishment, or payment of a curse?
And could its evil be put to rest with Bible and with verse?
The explanations that it spawned were fantastical and myriad.
And maybe the ultimate answer lies in Quartzite,
Under Hi-Jolly's pyramid.
Yet some believe the rider's ghost still roams the haunted land,
Seeking to reunite itself with the cadaverous caravan.
But to this day it remains unknown by this or any other mammal,
How and why that poor soul came to be strapped
'Crossed the back of that red-haired camel.

Petroglyph of a camel,
Red Tank Draw, Verde Valley

Little Bill

This is another true story, which mingles the involvements of Earl Van Deren and Ira Smith, (see <u>Ira and the Bad Cook</u>). Some of the other names mentioned in this piece have their own stories in Verde Valley history. The Purdymun family is mentioned in my <u>Bear Howard</u> poem. The numerous members of this family are said at one time or another to have homesteaded on every piece of flat ground along the length of Oak Creek Canyon. Earl Van Deren purchased an old hunting cabin which Jess Purdymun had built in Sterling Canyon. (For more on Charles Sterling, see <u>Justice, Revenge, and Memory: The Anatomy of a Killing</u>.) Earl and Ira disassembled the cabin, numbered the individual logs, and dragged them by mule south to the homestead Earl had taken over from Bill. This cabin is now on the National Registry of Historic Places. Bill Fredricks' name is also a matter of uncertainty. There is disagreement as to whether the last name was Fredrick or Fredricks, or Frederick or Fredericks. Some have said his actual first name was Henry. He is alleged to have signed a 1924 election poll as H. L. Fredricks. Earl is said to have spoken with Bill about eleven days before finding him dead in the cabin, and at the time of their last speaking, Bill seemed in normal health. Earl did not specify the identity of the friend that was with him when he found Bill. The actual circumstances of Bill's death remain an unsolved mystery.

Little Bill

The snow was never little Bill's friend, as each crippled step reminded him.

It had been that way ever since the day

That the town-bound train blindsided him.

Little Bill was a cowman, without a cowgirl to love him.

So he strove to make his own way, all five foot, two inches of him.

But I'll take pains to make it plain, even as this story begins,

That even though Bill lived alone, he still had lots of friends.

The cattle were moving along just fine on the trail outside of Flagstaff.

And Bill was thinking about wetting his whistle,

And having himself a few laughs.

When all of a sudden the sky turned black, and a blizzard overtook him.

And the trees turned white, and the temperature fell,

And the path of the trail forsook him.
But clever Bill found the railroad tracks,
And he knew they'd be his salvation.
And he turned his thoughts back to the whiskey glass
He would raise once his cattle were stationed.
But maybe that frozen blanket of white muffled the rail's vibration.
Or maybe his horse was under the spell of its rider's determination.
For the train struck them fully unaware, and the horse's death was instant.
But Bill dove into a drifted bank some three or four yards distant.

The engineer braked the train to a halt and begged Bill to get onboard.
"I couldn't see you because of the snow,
So you sure owe your life to the Lord!
Now let's get you to town so a doctor can see if you really are in one piece.
I can't leave you alone out here in this storm
Or you'll surely come to grief."
But Bill was angry and he threw out a string of words
Hot enough to melt ice.
And damned if the man who'd killed his horse was fit to offer him advice.
So Bill marched off through the mounded snow
And out of the engineer's sight.
And he made town alright, but the cost of his pride
Was to lose all his toes to frostbite.

The railroad never compensated Bill for his disability.
But Bill Fredricks wasn't the kind of man to wallow in self pity.
But a crippled man didn't stand much chance of taming a rugged land.
So Bill sold off his homestead rights, and gave up his ranching plans.
Earl Van Deren bought those rights, and helped to defray Bill's loss.
And Bill moved into a wooden shack on the east side of Dry Creek Wash.

Earl and his friend Ira Smith relocated Jess Purtymun's old cabin.
They disassembled and dragged the logs
Four miles down from Sterling Canyon.
The reassembled structure would serve as a cattleman's base.

And Ira, his wife Elsie, and their baby, lived with Earl there on the place.
When Elsie's sister came to stay and help her with the child,
Earl knew his bachelor days were up, and he became beguiled.
So the two best friends became brothers in law, married to beautiful sisters.
And they called their home the Honeymoon Place,
In spite of the splinters and blisters.

Earl ran his stock north of Soldier's Pass in the days of Prohibition.
And Bill used society's attitude to make a career transition.
Each month when he'd collect his check
From the Social Security Administration,
He'd hobble over to the bank and head for the teller's station.
In spite of his infirmity and the fact he was "over the hill,"
He always seemed to have the extra cash
To buy a new one hundred dollar bill.
And maybe it helped his self esteem or bolstered his fractured ego
That he wore a wad of those bills clipped to his overalls
When he'd come to town to meet his amigos.

And nobody had to wonder about the source of the extra cash.
They knew there were shadowy canyons
Where Bill kept his moonshine stashed.
Although it was banned by the law of the land in central Arizona,
If whiskey was their quest, men knew that the best
Came from Bill's still outside of Sedona.

But although the reputation of what he produced
Brought a measure of prosperity,
Where fate was concerned, Bill still hadn't earned
Very much in the way of charity.
The cabin he was living in caught fire and burned down.
And Earl told Bill to move back on over to his former homestead grounds.
Earl moved his family into town, installing Bill as the cabin's caretaker.
A satisfactory situation for a bootleg whiskey maker.
Rumor was Bill buried his cash in cans somewhere out near the cabin.
This was bound to be an invitation for something bad to happen.

Bill Fredericks (right) at the Van Deren cabin
Photo courtesy
Sedona Heritage Museum

One Christmastime, when he'd been out of touch, Earl drove out to see Bill.
And he stopped his truck to take a look from the crest of a nearby hill.
Bill's horse stood alone in the snowbound corral,
No smoke rose from the cabin's chimney.
But what would trouble Earl the most, at first he saw but dimly.
There were impressions in the snow that seemed to tell a story.
And Earl soon learned, the more he discerned,
The more he had cause to worry.

A vehicle had driven in from the main road,
And stopped where the cabin could be watched.
(Some would later suspect that the robbers had returned
 To the scene of the crime they had botched.)
The vehicle had driven away, but Earl knew something wasn't right.
On the snow covered ground, not far from the door,
He saw red upon the white.

Now Earl was glad he'd brought along a friend for company.
So they could both corroborate what they might be about to see.
No one answered to their calls. The horn honks faded into silence.
And both men hoped they weren't about to encounter a scene of violence.
On the frozen ground near the cabin's door, lay a bloodied length of rope.
This confirmed Earl's suspicions, and drained away his hope.
When they entered the unlocked cabin, Bill lay frozen on his cot.
Half of his head was covered with blood, 'though he had not been shot.
There were no signs of struggle. Everything seemed to be in order.
But if this was the work of enemies, they'd given Bill no quarter.

The coroner found a hole made by something blunt
On the back of poor Bill's head.
And a hammer was found lying on a shelf above the dead man's bed.
But a hundred dollars in cash was found
In the drawer of a nearby nightstand.
So maybe the robbers' tactics had turned more violent than they'd planned?
Maybe they couldn't make Bill talk, no matter what they tried,
And maybe those tracks were them coming back to see if Bill had died?
Ira Smith had another theory, that Bill had gotten sick,
And while trying to get the saddle on, he'd caused his horse to kick.
And the horse's hoof had caught him on the backside of his head,
And he'd managed to stagger back inside, and died there on his bed.

Whether it was murder or accident, the evidence proved inconclusive.
And if someone out there bears the guilt, they've managed to remain elusive.
The owner of the Oak Creek Tavern once gave an interview,
And claimed there were parts of the story that she alone now knew.
"But too much time has now gone by for it to make any difference.
And now the lines begin to blur between the truth and inference.
And even if I named some names and revealed some hidden facts,
The names would all be dead men, and none of it will bring Billy back."

And now even she is gone, without solving the mystery.
And Bill's life and death are a footnote in Sedona's history.
The cabin has suffered from vandals and the ravages of age.
'Though Hollywood once used it in Riders of the Purple Sage.
And Ira Smith played a cowboy who didn't have far to roam
As he acted scenes not far from the walls of his family's first home.

But in a cinematic irony so great even Bill's own ghost might swoon…
The last western to feature that cabin…was titled, Blood on the Moon.

Jack Duff's Bum Luck

This true story is told by Albert Thompson in <u>Those Early Days</u> (1968) under the title, "A Tragedy." Mr. Thompson guesses the ill-fated expedition took place sometime around 1905. The only name he could remember of any of the participants was Jack Duff, so whether he was one of the principal leaders of the expedition or not, Mr. Duff has become the protagonist in my poetic version of these events.

Jack Duff's Bum Luck

Ol' Jack Duff his luck was tough.
The expedition had gone fishin' with sufficient stuff.
Slabs of bacon, cans of beans,
Enough old newspapers to serve as the means,
Cornmeal, fryin' pans, even a camera for trophyin',
And several kinds of fruit pies, so the camp would be utopian.
They took just enough water for the first morning's coffee –
There'd be plenty more there, in the creek.
Because the bulk of the beverages on board for that week
Were the kind meant to separate the bold from the meek –
Cases of beer, and some "snake bite medicine".
So "Fish beware, or swim if you dare!"
Was the cry of these bold and intrepid men.

These "sporties" from Jerome had left their hillside home
In search of Oak Creek's tasty trout.
But their wagon's load on the Lime Kiln Road,
Cast that outcome into doubt.
At the height of the trail, well up above Spring Creek,
A neglected wheel gave out with a shriek,
And the wooden spokes began to shrink,
Tilting the wagon close to the brink.
The danger was obviously evident,

And some of the men got right reverent,
Blurting out their promises to heaven.

But ol' Jack Duff, his voice was gruff, as he shouted,
"Boys, enough's enough!
Those fish'll have to wait while we shift our freight.
So build a fire to heat the rim, and prop that axel on a shim –
For we'll never see our precious cargo again –
If it tumbles down this bluff!"
So they all hove to, and they all pitched in.
They were hale and hearty, determined men.
For the certain loss they'd sure lament – even if it came by accident –
Were those cases of beer and that "snake bite medicine".

"So watch out, you scaly Oak Creek veterans.
This time you'll find you're up against some better men.
And if this delay should take the whole day,
That'll be no cause to mutter.
By-n'-by you'll meet our flies,
And we'll acquaint you with lemon and butter!"

And it wasn't long before the glowing metal
Was wrapped around the wheel to settle.
And their spirits had returned to a finer fettle,
When awareness struck with the sting of a nettle –
The heated metal must be cooled with haste,
Or the spokes will drop from its embrace.
And the truth was plain to see there on everyone's face –
It was water that they were deficient in,
These otherwise quite well provisioned men.

Photo courtesy
Sedona Heritage
Museum

"Well I'll be sworn, that's just low-down mean!"
Jack cussed as he emptied out the coffee canteen,
While the hot metal hissed and spit out steam,
As if mocking the now despairing men.

"Well, it pains me to state, but it's fish or cut bait,
And, boys, I must admit I fear…
If we hope to make it out of here…
It'll cost us what we hold most dear…
To fix that wheel and get back underway again.
We'll have to sacrifice those cases of beer,
And prob'ly the snake bite medicine."

Well, sometimes a sportsman's fate can be cruel.
And sometimes roads don't deliver you
To the place of your fondest intention.
And our best laid plans might make us fools.
And sometimes survival's harshest rules
Will dictate restricted invention.
It wasn't a matter of life or death, except for the fish
(And they ain't holdin' their breath).
Just a matter of reputation.
And poles unbent and hooks left dry
Weren't enough to make these grown men cry.
Just another truncated vacation.
But there was no denyin' how it broke their hearts
To be deprived of the comfort of the brewers' arts –
Those cases of beer, and that "snake bite medicine".

So with a sigh and a moan our heroes headed home,
Fate had finally fixed their wagon.
'Though their hopes were denied, they would salvage some pride,
And the fish would be left to their braggin'.
They'd make up stories of exaggerated guile,
And their friends might wink and those fish might smile,
And joke about them rank and file,
But any sane man knows that trip just wouldn't have been worthwhile
Without those cases of beer and that "snake bite medicine".

The Art of Dueling

Arizona has had a long love affair with guns. They were an absolute necessity in the early days, but by the time of the Constitutional Convention of 1910, delegates like Albert Baker (a confederate veteran of the Civil War) were afraid that the territory's violent reputation would prevent it from gaining statehood, and attempted to distance themselves from these early associations with statements like, "Carrying arms is dangerous to oneself and to one's associates and should not be permitted under any circumstances. It is most dangerous and vile." This sentiment was echoed by delegate Wilfred Webb: "The carrying of weapons is a pernicious thing. We are no longer a frontier country." (Webb's statement may have been calculated to distance himself from his participation in the notorious Wham paymaster robbery of 1889.) William F. "Buffalo Bill" Cody, who was being touted as a senatorial candidate for the new state, said, "Arizona doesn't care how I stand on public questions as long as I am able to shoot straight." In its centennial year, Arizona's state legislature adopted the Colt Peacemaker as the Official State Gun, and passed a law making it legal to carry a loaded firearm into a bar! A proposed law allowing students and professors to carry weapons on Arizona's college campuses was defeated.

There are two parts to this story, and both of them are true. Sylvester Mowry was one of the earliest advocates for Arizona to be granted territorial status. He favored calling everything south of the Gila River "Arizona Territory." He was sent by the citizens of Tubac to lobby congress as an unofficial delegate. (Nathan P. Cook was the official delegate elected by the citizens of Tucson.) A lieutenant in the American army, and owner of the wealthy Patagonia mines in Arizona's Sonoita Valley, Mowry was unhappy with the lack of attention received from federal representatives at Santa Fe, and with the removal of federal troops from Forts Bowie and Buchanan, which left his operations and the lives of his employees and neighbors vulnerable to depredations of the marauding Apaches. Thus Mowry, along with numerous other influential citizens of what would eventually become southern Arizona, saw the rising Confederacy as a more tangible hope for recognition and protection. Colonel Edward Cross, owner and editor of <u>The Arizonian</u>, the first newspaper in the territory, saw Mowry's endorsement of the Confederacy as treason. Their duel has been documented, and it is claimed that in its aftermath the entire contents of a forty-seven gallon barrel of liquor was consumed by the participants and spectators. Within two weeks of the duel, Mowry's supporters purchased <u>The Arizonian</u> and altered its editorial point of view. Cross would later be killed in action at the battle of Gettysburg. Mowry's mine holdings were confiscated by General Carleton when he declared martial law after bringing the troops of his

California Column into Tucson in 1863. After the war, Mowry successfully sued the United States government and was awarded compensation of about $40,000, although his mines were valued at well over one million dollars. He later died in England. Accounts of the Mowry-Cross feud can be found in <u>All Hell Needs is Water</u>, by Budge Ruffner, and in <u>The Far Southwest 1846-1912, A Territorial History</u>, by Howard Roberts Lamar.

Robert Groom came to Arizona following the early gold discoveries in the Bradshaw Mountains. A confederate veteran, he called his homestead "Groomville." The initial party of federally appointed officials under Territorial Governor John N. Goodwin stayed at Groom's place while reconnoitering the newly designated Territory in 1863. As a surveyor, Groom laid out the first grid work of streets for the newly declared capital at Prescott, and went on to serve as a delegate in two sessions of the Territorial Legislature. The anecdote about his duel is cited from the memoirs of Prescott Judge John J. Hawkins by Leo W. Banks in <u>Rattlesnake Blues, Dispatches from a Snakebit Territory</u>.

The Art of Dueling

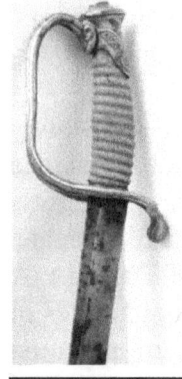

Cavalryman's sword, Fort Verde

In those bold and bloody days of the Arizona Territory,
A prudent man kept his gun near at hand.
It was considered mandatory.
For the need to avenge one's honor was frequently insistent.
And the presence of the law out there was rare to non-existent.
And grievances must be addressed
In the absence of a judge's ruling.
So the custom of the day required
There'd be some occasional dueling.

The pen is mightier than the sword, or so the saying goes.
And a newspaper editor might use his pen to denigrate his foes.
An opinionated journalist might think he has a shield,
And can't be held accountable or summoned to the field.
And so it was that Colonel Ed Cross, under the "Arizonian's" masthead,
Fired salvo after salvo until Sylvester Mowry's reputation had been blasted.
But West Point graduate Mowry was a man of action,
So he specified the place and time to demand his satisfaction.

As the challenged party, Colonel Cross chose Burnside rifles.
(But secretly regretted he'd used harsh words
                as though they were mere trifles.)
The wind blew fiercely across the plain as they squared off at forty paces.
And 'though both men probably had second thoughts,
It didn't show on their faces.
But the first rounds both flew wide of their marks,
In spite of their murderous plans.
And maybe the wind was to blame for that (or maybe it was shaky hands).

And now Colonel Cross squinted down the sights, and took a careful aim.
And he prayed that this would be the shot to end this deadly game.
But this bullet too took a wild path, bound for parts unknown.
And unscathed Mowry had a second chance to make the Colonel atone.
So again he leveled his Burnside, and sighted down the barrel.
And Cross lamented those diatribes that had brought him to this peril.
And for a moment the wind let up, and everyone held their breath.
They knew they were about to bear witness
To the Colonel's imminent death.
But at the final instant, Mowry fired into the air.
And the startled spectators knew they'd witnessed something rare.
As the injured party, killing his tormentor would have been fair.
But the title of cold-blooded killer was one Mowry did not choose to wear.
So all the boys trooped back to town. No longer would they bicker.
Instead they let their anger drown in a barrelful of liquor.

But maybe the weirdest duel of all was fought near old Fort Whipple.
'Though in the papers of the day it hardly made a ripple.
But even if the reporters of the day didn't consider it much of a story,
It's said that this one ended the custom of dueling in the Arizona Territory.

It was a time when lines were drawn, and not just in the sand.
And some were the kind that if you crossed, your life was in your hands.
Southern pride still burned in the heart of a certain ex-confederate –
Old Robert Groom, who surveyed the grid for the capitol at Prescott.

Memories of rebel loss filled his yesterdays, todays, and tomorrows.
So it's no surprise that old man Groom would often drown his sorrows.
One day when he was in his cups, three officers from the fort
Disparaged the valor of the South,
And Groom made a sharp retort.
The soldiers threw their gauntlets down,
But the old surveyor surprised them:
"I'll whip all three of you Yankee dogs!"
Then he spat, just to show he despised them.

When the officers kept their rendezvous
At the place that Groom had selected,
They wore their dress parade uniforms,
Not a detail was neglected.

Soldier's parade helmet, late 19th century

Their boots were highly polished, and the mid-day sun
Gleamed off their bright brass buttons, and their freshly oiled guns.
Ostrich plumes danced jauntily on the hats cocked on their heads.
And although it was noon, their coats were festooned
With braids and epaulets.
And they weren't surprised to find that Groom seemed unprepared for battle.
As he drunkenly waved and propped himself up,
Leaning on two old wooden paddles.
"No wonder those Johnny-Rebs lost the war,"
They laughed as they closed the distance.
"We'll splinter those paddles with our swords if he offers any resistance!"
"The old man's been out in the sun too long! His brains are surely addled.
That bearded freak is up the creek,
And he's brought along his own two paddles!"
"That drunken reb's as good as dead, he's come like a lamb to the slaughter.
He can't avoid the fight by taking flight – 'cause there isn't any water!"

Their laughter echoed across the field and made them sound quite giddy.
'Though if old Groom refused to yield, they'd shoot him without pity.
They didn't consider this adversary as being very wise.
And in their glee, they paid no heed to the buzzing clouds of flies.

But as their course brought them downwind, the air assaulted their nostrils
With a penetrating stench that burned their eyes,
And grabbed them by the tonsils.
And as the old man stepped aside, their eyes beheld a sight
That brought the bile up to their lips, and drained their faces white.
They stood there trying not to breathe. Their feet had lost all traction.
Before them lay the corpse of a rotting bull –
A steaming mound of putrefaction.

"I've no desire to take your lives," Groom told his retching foes.
"But I am the challenged party, and this is what I chose.
We're going to use these here paddles to shovel the guts from that bull.
And if your pile is bigger than mine, I'll apologize in full.
And in the spirit of fair play, I'll let you all go first!
If y'all can keep your breakfast down, you can make me eat my words."

By now the sweating officers were turning rather green.
And as far as upholding their honor went, they were no longer keen.
They'd come with the expectation that they'd leave covered in glory.
But Groom's plan threatened to cover them
With something disgustingly gory.
And so the soldiers quit the field without ever firing a gun.
And their retreat was reminiscent of the Battle of Bull Run.

Now it's said these events went on to prevent
The custom of dueling thereafter.
For when hot-headed fools would lose their cool,
This story turned anger to laughter.
No matter the degree of hostility behind the instigation,
The recollection of this humiliation diffused the situation.
So if there is a moral we might draw from all this history,
It might be best if we addressed our differences creatively.
But the ultimate lesson we should take away from all this schooling,
Is that it's always best to just try to avoid the so-called civilized art of dueling.

Why Arizona Doesn't Have a Seaport

This is another of those semi-persistent historical anecdotes that is sometimes cited to explain the odd shape of Arizona's southern border with Mexico. It's also another case of the facts getting in the way of an otherwise good story.

John Bartlett, a merchant from Rhode Island, had wanted to be appointed an ambassador. He was instead offered the post of commissioner for the U.S.-Mexico border expedition, charged with establishing the new international border in the aftermath of the United States' acquisition of what had been the entire northern half of Mexico at the conclusion of the Mexican-American War in 1848. Bartlett was a well educated and highly cultured man who was said to have the ability to relate to and be on easy terms with all manner of men. Although well-versed in astronomy, zoology, geology, and ethnography, he had no prior experience in surveying or diplomacy. By most accounts he is believed to have been out-maneuvered by his Mexican counterpart General Pedro Garcia Conde', who convinced him to work from a map that everyone knew was inaccurate and that effectively ceded about 6,000 square miles of territory back to Mexico. The expedition was staffed by some one hundred or so "adventurers" who saw it as an opportunity to get themselves transported to the California goldfields at government expense. Bartlett's brother was appointed quartermaster to the expedition and wasted thousands of dollars on weevil infested flour and worm infested pork. Bartlett actually devoted the majority of his energies to compiling notes for a book about the cultural and natural history of the American southwest. The scholarship of this work is still highly respected today. Support for the boundary project in the U.S. Congress was lukewarm at best for a number of reasons. Some felt that the United States had instigated the war as a pretext for a land grab justified by the doctrine of "Manifest Destiny". Some feared that the South would gain direct access to California via a railroad line through the new territory, and that this would spread southern influence resulting in more congressional delegates in favor of slavery. (This is also a prime reason why Arizona was not granted official status as a United States Territory until 1863.) And many inside and outside the halls of Congress felt that the sun-scorched lands south of the Camino Del Muerto (Road of Death) were so bereft of value that the border expedition amounted to a huge joy ride at taxpayer expense. (The region's gold, silver, and copper resources were yet to be revealed.) The eventual congressional strategy was to simply allow the expedition to exhaust its funding and supplies, thus forcing the abandonment of its unfinished work. When it was realized that this had prevented the country from acquiring a viable railroad route, James Gadsden was dispatched in 1853 to negotiate the purchase of enough land from Mexico to make this feasible. Due to the recent, ill-fated "invasion" of Mexican territory by William Walker and his makeshift "army" which had unsuccessfully attempted to seize the Baja Peninsula, the Mexican government was disposed to sell only the minimum amount of its territory that would prevent another invasion by legitimate United States forces.

Lieutenant Amiel Whipple's services to the Arizona Territory were honored with Fort Whipple being named for him (see "Kissin' Jenny" and "The Art of Dueling"). The unpopularity of this chapter of American history is perhaps summed up by the fact that even as prestigious a senator as General Sam Houston of Texas was unable to get Bartlett's two volume account of his experiences (containing, among other noteworthy scientific observations, the compilation of working vocabularies of twenty different Indian tribes of the region) introduced into the Congressional Record. In a break with tradition regarding official records of previous expeditions of this kind, the government declined to publish it, leaving Bartlett to do so at his own expense, which he did under the title, A Personal Narrative of Explorations and Incidents in Texas, New Mexico, California, Sonora, and Chihuahua, Connected with the United States and Mexican Boundary Commission, 1850-1853.

Why Arizona Doesn't Have a Seaport

When it comes to motivation, the tried and true art of gentle persuasion
Won't always get you where you need to go.
If your goal is to inspire, you can manipulate desire,
Or love or fame, to change the status quo.
Then of course there's always money –
You catch more flies when using honey.
Ego is useful for heightening the competition.
Awakening a sense of pride can swing the victory to your side.
Especially if yours is a nationalistic mission.
Revenge is popular of course, for those who act without remorse,
And long to make their enemies squirm or bleed.
But when it's all been said and done, the surest webs that have been spun
Rely upon that champion motive, greed.
There've been dozens of desperate despots specializing in coercion and fear.
But if you really want to get things done, don't turn your back on beer.

They were surveying the Mexican boundary line,
Down south of the Camino Del Muerto.
Where there's nothing but heat and burning sand,
And the devil's wind playing a scherzo.
Commissioner Bartlett had gone on hiatus.
He was absent for forty-four days,
While his men labored under a solar sadist
That baked them with withering rays.
"We fought a war with Mexico to win this land,"
General Sherman cracked.
"And we should fight another war with them to make them take it back!"
The famous scout Kit Carson composed Arizona a sonnet.
He described it as "so barren and empty, that a wolf could not live on it."

Still they pushed their line ever westward, on toward the Gulf of Baja.
Between the cactus thorns and the rattlesnakes,
Every one of them missed his mama.
Some had come for the adventure, some were there to make a name.
Some saw it as their ticket to a California goldrush claim.
When it came to the surveying they were wet behind the ears,
But their accuracy was the responsibility of the Topographical Engineers.
As long as they held their flags in place, everything would work out fine.
They'd only been asked to accomplish the task
Of plotting a simple, straight line.

But then Lieutenant Colonel Graham, the expedition's "Astronomer Royal,"
Initiated mayhem, and said things that made their blood boil.
"To claim the mouth of the Colorado River," he said,
"Is an injudicious arrangement. It might give offense to Mexico,
And cause us some estrangement."
His military understanding seemed at best a little weedy.
But maybe he didn't know we'd won the war?
Maybe he hadn't read the treaty.
His arguments about rank and position brought the work to a grinding halt.
'Though Bartlett's failure to take control was also much at fault.

The workers knew it was up to them to get themselves out of this mess.
Their leadership was paralyzed and the government couldn't care less.
Suspicious northern senators didn't want to help the south.
Only Emory and Whipple seemed to care about reaching the river's mouth.
What with Bartlett's absence and ineptitude and Graham's lack of vision,
The men didn't feel they should take the heat
For Washington's lack of precision.
Their patriotism wasn't fired, and if the truth be known,
The only mouths they cared about were in fact their own.
Their consciences wouldn't bother them over jobs they were neglecting,
If they could only be cut loose so they could go prospecting.
These frustrated men didn't know very much about the halls of Montezuma,
But they'd got word that hundreds of barrels of beer
Had been delivered to the saloons at Yuma.
"Bartlett only cares about writing his book,
And that Colonel is really an ass."
"The collision of science and politics has created this impasse."
"The path to the sea is obstructed, boys. This plan is in need of revision!"
So they turned their transits northwestward.
They made their own decision.

And when they reached the river at Yuma, they crowded up to the bar.
Congress had killed their funding,
But they'd hitched their wagons to another star.
They had no patience for military bluster, and no respect for political agility.
The only thing that passed muster was their own navigational ability.
They'd followed their own wing-ding. They'd drawn a line in the sand.
They would not be held responsible for Washington's half-assed plan.
And now that it was over, they raised their glasses in a toast.
But they didn't make grandiose speeches or engage in gratuitous boasts.
They'd done what had been asked of them. Their duty they did not shirk.
Their leaders had failed, but they had prevailed.
And it was close enough for government work.

There are holes in the Indian blanket, there's a crack in the Liberty Bell.

And many a good intention has paved the road to hell.

If by relating these circumstances, I've challenged your world view,

Well I admit it's a heck of a story, but only some of it's true.

Arizona would most likely have a seaport under terms of the Mexican Cession.

So why it didn't get one remains a valid question.

Who's responsible for this fiasco? How was it allowed to happen?

Why did we have to buy more land in that purchase negotiated by Gadsden?

A system of political patronage is one underlying reason.

And the Lieutenant Colonel's tantrums

Would seem to have bordered on treason.

Bartlett was clearly in over his head and his Mexican counterpart was clever.

But Major Emory and Lieutenant Whipple

Did yeoman's service in this endeavor.

That Congress left the expedition high and dry is another part that's true.

But the reason the border veers northwest has nothing to do with brew.

It's natural that someone would've concocted such a colorful explanation,

But surveyors dying for a drink was fermented from imagination.

Yet the fact there are some who've believed it

Makes one thing abundantly clear:

Some men will do practically anything if they think it will get them a beer.

The Saga of John Munds and the Tragic Double Murder of 1899

When Arizona was organized as a United States Territory in 1863, Yavapai County incorporated the entire northern half of the land within its boundaries. (Not including Pah-Ute County, which was re-drawn as the southern triangle of Nevada that same year and re-named Clark County.) This was the largest county anywhere in America, earning it the moniker "The Mother of All Counties". Coconino County, America's second largest county today, was incorporated out of Yavapai County land in 1893. The northern half of the valley of the Verde River lies within Yavapai County's boundaries today.

William Munds brought his family into the Verde Valley in 1876. He operated a butcher shop in Jerome and in 1899 he was elected as the city's first mayor. Today around north-central Arizona there are place names like Munds Park (the family's summer homestead), Munds Mountain, Munds Canyon, the Old Munds Highway, and the Munds Wagon Trail, which became the basis for the present-day Schnebly Hill Road. John Munds was a very popular and effective sheriff of Yavapai County. He married Frances Willard, who rose to prominence in the National Women's Suffragist Movement. She was the first woman elected to the Arizona Legislature, and only the second woman in America to attain such an office. Neal Munds was eighteen years old when he accepted a dare from some cowboys at Willard Springs (the Willard family's summer homestead) to attempt to ride a wild bronc that no one had been able to tame. Witnesses said that the horse's initial buck snapped Neal's neck so violently that he was surely already dead, but his body remained in the saddle as the crazed horse plunged itself into a tree, killing itself as well. Myron Carrier is believed to have been the first civilian doctor to practice medicine in the Verde Valley. His killing of a black bear in a pool at the bottom of Bear Wallow Canyon was the canyon's name-sake event.

The Wingfield family also came to the Verde Valley in 1876. In Pioneer Stories of Arizona's Verde Valley, both Clint Wingfield and Mack Rogers are described as exemplary citizens and men of sterling qualities who always stood for what was good and upright. Their murder is still considered by many Verde Valley citizens to be the worst tragedy in Camp Verde's history. (Tom Ketchum actually shot Clint Wingfield in the back, but "chest" made a better rhyme for "desk".) "Cap'n Boyd" was a Yavapai who had retired from service with the Indian Scouts stationed at Fort Verde (now the town of Camp Verde.) John Munds, together with Ed and Frank Wingfield, spent the better part of a year trailing Black Jack. At one point they came upon his abandoned campsite and found a note he'd left for them: "Boys, I know you are after me. I'll be back in two or three hours and if not, I'll be four miles north, gathering bees." When Munds presented his extradition papers in New Mexico, the U.S. Marshal there refused to accept them. Ketchum's arm had been blown off by a shotgun blast, and it was feared he would not survive the trip back to Arizona for trial. At Black Jack's hanging, a bag was placed over his head, and pinned to the shoulders and collar of his jacket. The noose was not properly adjusted, and when the trap door was released, Black Jack's head was separated from his body. The bag was the only thing that kept the head from rolling off of the gallows platform. The doctor who had been assigned to officiate at the hanging earned some extra money by agreeing to sew the head back on before burial.

Once, following a performance of my show "Voices of the Verde" at the Sedona Heritage Museum, an elderly Mexican gentleman who had been in the audience told me that his grandfather, while a young man in New Mexico, had been hired to run errands for the hotel where Black Jack was being kept while awaiting hanging. Ketchum had apparently taken a liking to the young Mexican. "Emilio," he told him, "you be sure to be here when that pretty senorita brings my dinner from the restaurant. She is a sight to be seen." As recommended, the young man was there at the appointed time and, as promised, the girl was a beauty. Ketchum introduced the two. They attended his hanging as their first date. "A lot of people don't like Black Jack," the old gentleman told me, "but in *mi familia*, we don't see him as such a bad guy."

The Saga of John Munds
And the Tragic Double Murder of 1899

Old William Munds, he had
   three sons and a daughter
   named Melvina.
She became a bride
   at Doctor Carrier's side.
"She's a beauty," you'd say,
   if you'd seen her.

John Munds, Melvina, Myron & Iva Carrier. Photo courtesy Sedona Heritage Museum:

To the boys fate was fickle, and the Grim Reaper's sickle
Too early took two of the trio.
'Though their father found fame 'midst the copper mine claims
On the western side of the rio.
Young Neal ran his course on the back of a horse
He was determined to be made no plowboy.
His acceptance of dare was as devil-may-care
As befitted a reckless, wild cowboy.
But that horse was insane and it battered their brains
On the limbs of an ancient tree.
And Death's cruel saw began to gnaw on the limbs of the Munds family.

Returning one day to the family corral,
Young John Munds found bad Jimmy Wilson.
His intentions were clear from the rope in his hand.
He was there in the role of a villain.
"You just hold my reins, son, while I catch a fresh horse,"
The rustler said with distain.
"But that horse is mine," the boy replied. "You raise your hands skyways."
Now Wilson had dabbled in robbery, and attempted a series of rapes,
And had made himself a wanted man through a string of local scrapes.
And he didn't figure this boy on the horse had the sand to end his run,
So he dropped his rope, and with his last act, he went for his six-gun.
But John was fast and his rifle's blast laid that bad man to rest.
Time in its way would prove that this day
Foretold of the star on John's chest.

Elder brother Jim built the Old Munds Trail,
Famed shortcut through Bear Wallow Canyon.
But another tragic accident left Hattie Loy without her companion.
One day after bringing his stock to the pen,
Jim leaned from the saddle and took hold
Of the barrel of the rifle that he'd left by the gate.
From there different stories unfold.

The gun maybe slipped, or hammer struck fence,
Putting a bullet into his head.
And by the time doctor Carrier arrived from Jerome,
Jim Munds was long since dead.
They buried him up there on the mountain place,
Where soon they'd bury Neal.
But death stayed near, and that same year, Melvina lost her baby girl.
But the living must eat, and William Munds sold meat
To the miners in hungry Jerome.
They rewarded his fare by making him mayor of their fire-ravaged home.
And son John became Sheriff and he served with honor,
In Yavapai, the mother of all counties.
From Prescott to Flagstaff his name brought fear
To men on the run from their bounties.
But the lowest days of his long career
From the Bradshaws to Canyon Diablo,
Were the months he spent trailing a man called Black Jack,
A murderous desperado.

It was just after the meeting
Where they planned for the Fourth,
Down at the abandoned post of Fort Verde,
That a stranger had lingered near the Sutler's store
As Mack Rogers closed in no hurry.
Old Cap'n Boyd would later tell
Of how he had heard Mack run,
And the startling sound of the stranger's shot
That dropped Mack, as he reached for his gun.
The stranger had said, "Stop Mack, this won't do",
Before he'd shot his victim.

Doors on the old sutler's store, Camp Verde

But to this day, there's no one sure just why his killer picked him.

When he heard the clap of the gun's report,
Clint Wingfield sprang from his desk.
But another blast of the stranger's gun put a bullet in Clint's chest.

And then the killer turned and ran, not pausing to search for treasure.
"I'll kill you all!" he screamed in the street.
And put a bullet in Cap'n Boyd's leg for good measure.

Mack's death had been swift, but Clint held on with grit
'Til his brothers arrived at his side.
They stayed with him in vigil there. It was around midnight he died.
Clint babbled incoherently about playing in some sort of ball game.
"Open the windows, I'm smothering," he said when death's final call came.
John Munds and the posse took up the chase.
They could read the killer's course.
He'd spurred his unshod mount so hard that blood had run from the horse.
But they lost him down around Mud Tanks, where he blended in with a herd.
Then a month was lost chasing futile leads, and most of the posse returned.
But Munds and the Wingfield brothers flat refused to give it up.
They'd learned that they were on the trail of a man called Charlie Bishop.
Munds heard of a prisoner in New Mexico,
Who'd been wounded while robbing a train.
And given his description, he and Bishop seemed the same.
When interviewed, the man confessed to being the one they chased.
But he would not admit his involvement in the Verde murder case.
He claimed his name was Tom Ketchum, and his alias was Black Jack.
And John Munds returned without the man who shot down Clint and Mack.

We may long for justice or vengeance, like a balm to soothe our hate.
But it's like that Russian Tolstoy wrote: "God sees the truth, but waits."
When they hanged Black Jack in New Mexico,
The noose snapped his head from his body.
But that didn't ease the Rogers family's pain,

Or the Wingfields' melancholy.
Some say life's ruled by accident.
Others claim death cancels worry.
God grant us strength and courage then,
As we struggle on our journey.

Medical officers' surgical instruments at Ft. Verde.

Bear Howard

John Jefferson Howard was the second Anglo settler to take up residence in Oak Creek Canyon. He was a big man, well over six feet tall, and of a stature that seems to have attracted mythic properties to him. I once heard his grand-daughter say of him, "There are a lot of stories about Grandpa Howard. Some of them are true, and some of them are not so true." His daughter Martha is alleged to have disavowed the story about bringing him a file hidden in a cake, and at least one historian claims he was twice released from jail, rather than ever escaping. (His grand-daughter said the second release was motivated by the guards' pity for his age.) But the fact that he adopted the alias of "Charlie Smith" certainly seems to imply that he was worried about his true identity rendering him liable for prosecution. It has also been alleged that he was not six feet, eight inches tall as has been claimed, but one of the most famous photographs of him shows him to be easily the tallest of the crowd that stands with him. Some have claimed that the insolent cowboys he beat up were from the infamous Hashknife Outfit (the Aztec Land and Cattle Company), but Fred Piper of the Piper Ranch family told me that they were actually CO Bar hands (the Babbit Brothers Cattle Company). Since Fred grew up in Oak Creek's red rock country, I've gone with his authority on that. Despite his fearsome appearance and reputation, it is said that Bear Howard was a loving grandfather.

Given the difficulty of separating fact from fiction regarding his life, it is safe to say that J.J./"C.S."/"Bear" Howard was truly one of the region's most daunting characters.

Steven Purtymun family
Photo courtesy
Sedona Heritage Museum

Bear Howard

In early California days the Mexicans were dispossessed
Of the lands they'd held in Nuevo Spain
As the Anglos pushed their borders west.
J.J. Howard ran his stock not far from Sacramento.
From the Mexican war his shoulder bore a four inch lead memento.
Sheepherders began to encroach upon his horses' pasture.
And Jesse made it known that to continue that course
Would be flirting with disaster.

Since the death of his wife, the pride of his life
Were his son Jess, and his daughter Martha.
One day while Jesse was away from home,
Some Indians made the children their target.
J.J. and his friends foiled their plans by taking a seldom used trail.
As the gun battle raged on into the night,
The Indians knew their plan had failed.
The children were thrown onto cactus when the Indians sensed defeat.
And the would-be kidnappers used the moonless night to cover their retreat.

Another time Jesse returned to find an interloper's flock.
And then he heard someone laughing from on top of a nearby rock.
Jesse raised his rifle as anger clouded his sight.
And when the smoke cleared, the sheepherder's body
Had fallen from that height.
Jesse went to the sheriff and admitted to the murder.
'Though in his defense he said he'd only meant
To frighten the laughing herder.
But when the case came up for trial, the verdict went against him.
He told the judge it was an accident,
But the argument failed to convince him.
The court found intent in the sheepherder's death,
'Though Jesse felt the law had scorned him.
But to tell the truth, he was no longer sure
If that shot was only meant to warn him.

They sent him off to serve his time in the prison called San Quentin.
But when Martha came to visit him, she came there on a mission.
Martha believed her father had been given a bad break.
So she brought a present for him – a file inside a cake.
J.J. was quick when it came to leavin' – one less for the prison's quota.
And he followed Martha and her husband Stephen on their way to Arizona.

As a wanted man, Jesse stayed off-trail, and kept well out of sight.
He'd hunt game for the family's meals and bring it into camp at night.
They came to a massacred settlement on the banks of the Colorado River.
The bloodied, arrow-riddled corpses caused Martha to shiver.
Soon after they crossed the water, they encountered an army patrol.
And Jesse knew he'd best not tell the truth, lest he fall under their control.
So he avoided recapture, perhaps by a whisker's width.
When they asked him what his name was, he told them, "Charlie Smith."

"Mr. Smith" wandered up to Flagstaff.
He'd decided to do some more killing.
He knew there were bears and lions there, and he was more than willing.
And thanks to his great hunting skill, his fortunes were on the mend.
The venison and bear meat he supplied made him the butchers' best friend.
He reduced the predator population at every opportunity.
His success at this occupation made him a pillar of the community.
To earn himself a living he was called upon to shoot,
But for his recreation he liked to "get on a little toot."
His hunting dogs were his best friends, but if he was feeling frisky,
He liked to make the acquaintance of a bottle or two of whiskey.

One day in a saloon in Prescott, Jesse's tongue was loose and loud,
And he bragged that the day he killed that Mexican
Was a day that made him proud.
After he had sobered up, he regretted his indiscretion
As he found that he was prison bound, thanks to his drunken confession.
But the guards at the San Quentin Prison took pity on the old man,
So they left a horse by an unlocked door, and once again Jesse ran.

This time Jesse sought a place where he'd be left alone,
And he found what he was looking for at the base of the Mogollon.
Red rock cliffs and towering pines would shield him from detection.
Its remoteness and isolation would prevent the law's inspection.
So "C.S. Howard" returned to his work of ridding the region of bears.
And Martha and Stephen Purtymun came to join him there.

In picking up where he'd left off, Jesse was very proficient.
When it came to trapping and killing bears, no one else was so efficient.
The local stockmen thought of him as something of a savior.
And they were quite supportive of his mercenary behavior.
He chose a job that few would want, and fewer still would dare.
So they held him in high regard, and everyone called him "Bear."

Bear Howard (center) with dogs and admirers. Photo courtesy Sedona Heritage Museum

A few days after the sixty-seventh anniversary of his birth,
Bear was in a Flagstaff saloon, trying to quench his thirst.
He was having a private party with a few of his eighty-proof friends,
When some cowhands from the CO Bar got a notion in their heads.
They thought it would be funny to make the old man dance,
So one pulled out his pistol and told Bear he had one chance.
As the bullets started splintering the boards around his feet
Bear began to shuffle, which the cowboys found a treat.
They were convulsed with laughter, the gunman wore a grin.
'Til Bear brought his size sixteen boot up under the cowboy's chin.

It took almost thirty stitches to repair that cowboy's face.
The dancing Bear's high-steppin' knocked his jaw clean out of place.
And then old Bear was on him, and mixed with the victim's moans
His friends were stunned and sickened by the crunching of his bones.
And then the old man turned toward them, his fists were huge and bloody.
He asked, "Who'll be the next to dance?"
But their spines had turned to putty.
They scraped and bruised each other trying to squeeze out through the door.
And they left their honor lying with their friend there on the floor.

Bear married the widow Elizabeth James when he was more than seventy.
A union that attained some fame, if only for its brevity.
Some say it was Bear's dirty hunting dogs, and the smell of uncured hides
That pushed Elizabeth to the limit beyond which no love abides.
Some men always seem to fall victim to fortune's twists and bends,
And Jesse always seemed to have his share of needy friends.
He took pity on the hungry; he felt compassion for the lonely.
But his generosity of spirit cost him his matrimony.
His wife renounced her feelings, and she took back her vows.
She would no longer tolerate him giving away her cows.

After fifty-four years, Bear finally grew tired
Of the bullet he carried in his shoulder.
And he told a surgeon to take it out before he got much older.
The doctor wasn't keen to operate because he feared for his life.
His patient stood well over six feet tall and carried a very sharp knife!
Without a few stout men to hold Bear down the procedure might be risky.
But Bear assured him he'd remain calm after he'd drunk enough whiskey.
In the absence of an anesthetic, Bear drained the contents of a jug.
And so the doctor set to work, and extracted the Mexican slug.
Jesse endured the procedure, and maintained his good cheer.
And the doctor, in addition to his fee, kept the bullet as a souvenir.

Bear's eight grandchildren were a source of his recurring joy.
And he took the time to pass on his skills to the older Purtymun boys.
Grandson Dan once came with him to hunt lions on the Rim.
The only lions Bear caught that time were on the mornings Dan slept in.
Lions have good hearing and they know when someone's coming.
So Bear stressed a code of silence whenever they were hunting.
But Dan had trouble keeping quiet, even when he was tryin'.
So those mornings when little Dan slept in were bad luck for those lions.

Well into his nineties, Bear's health began to fade.
It was rare for a man in those days to see his ninth decade.
Rheumatoid arthritis, hard play and hard labor
Finally made him realize that Death was a not-too-distant neighbor.
Around Christmas time in 1910,
He decided to visit Martha and the grandchildren.
He climbed into his wagon, but at the south end of the track,
He reigned in the mules and, with a sigh, he took a long look back.
Did he know his time was almost up? Did he sense it even then?
Did he know that he would never see his beloved canyon again?
At Martha's house on Mingus Mountain, only a few days later,
Old Bear "went west" for the last time, to meet with his Creator.

The day would come when "civilization" would pacify these lands.
But in the day of old Bear Howard nature was tamed with calloused hands.
Purtymuns carved out a living from every flat place along Oak Creek.
Such a thing would not have been possible if they had been too meek.
It took courage and ability, and the Purtymuns had their share.
And for some of it they're beholdin' to the legacy of old Bear.
In death he's beyond capture or care of how history may show him.
But in life he was of a stature rare, and it took three names to know him.

Tarnished Star

In May of 1882, President Chester A. Arthur threatened to declare martial law over the Arizona Territory unless it showed more respect for law and order. His statement was largely triggered by events in Cochise County. Arizona's reputation for lawlessness and violence was one of the main reasons it was not granted statehood until 1912.

This true story is even more involved than I've described it. Several weeks after Billy Stiles turned on his pals, he walked into the jail one morning, shot the jailer in the leg, released Alvord and at least one of the other gang members, but left Bill Downing locked in his cell. Alvord and Stiles hid out in Mexico, where they were eventually contacted by Burt Mossman, captain of the Arizona Rangers, who convinced them to assist him in apprehending the notorious Augustine Chacon. In return for their help, Mossman would do what he could to see that they received light sentences for their robberies and jailbreak. Alvord and Stiles accepted the deal, but later dug their way out of the Tombstone jail. Alvord was apprehended and served a term in the Yuma Territorial Prison. Stiles escaped to Nevada, changed his name, and was later killed in a gunfight. Matt Burts served his time, then returned to Willcox and worked as a cowboy on his brother's ranch. Downing served ten years in prison before returning to Willcox where he operated a den of prostitutes and thieves called the Free and Easy Saloon. Downing's temper wasn't mollified by his time behind bars, and his open defiance of legal authority finally resulted in Arizona Ranger Billy Speed being sent to Willcox to rein him in. On an August morning in 1908, Speed stood in the street in front of the saloon and called for Downing to come out. As Downing made for the back door, someone slipped his revolver from its holster without him noticing. Downing went out the door, rounded the corner and was confronted by Speed coming the other way. In response to Speed's command to "throw up his hands," Downing reached for his gun, only to discover its untimely absence. Speed killed him with a single shot.

In a "small world" side note, the person labeled with the number 13 in the Bear Howard photograph on page 86, has been identified as "Three-Fingered Jack" and may be the same Jack Dunlap who appears in this story.

Tarnished Star

Burt Alvord wasn't the brightest mind that ever wore a star.
But with a gun he was the fearless kind, whose fame spread near and far.
He was deputized by John Slaughter, sheriff of the county of Cochise,
And sent to Pearce and Willcox, to provide them some relief.
And soon the raucous miners were keeping to the straight and narrow.
They kept their tempers well in check when playing at monte or faro.

Alvord was a prankster, who liked to make folks laugh.
Like the time the Tombstone citizens thought they'd read his epitaph.
The telegram said "Burts' and Alvord's bodies
Will arrive on the Bisbee stage."
And their friends wept to think there'd be no tomorrows
As they all convened to drown their sorrows
At the bullet-riddled bar in the gloom of the old Birdcage.
Remembrances were spoken, and testimonials were given.
Coffins were assembled, and nails were sadly driven,
And holy words were read from a Bible's tear-stained page.
But when that moribund stage rolled in,
Burts and Alvord alighted to flout 'em.
"We're awfully attached to our bodies," they said.
"And we never go anywhere without 'em!"

Alvord made friends easily, across the social spectrum.
But five there were especially, whose temperaments seemed to infect him.
There was deputy constable Billy Stiles,
Matt Burts, and mean Bill Downing.
"Three Finger Jack" Dunlap and Bravo Juan Yoas
Also supported his clowning.
Now Alvord and his associates weren't known for cogitation,
But Burt had stumbled on a plan to provide remuneration.

He could exploit his office and concoct an explanation,
And his sheriff's badge would be their shield,
And should their misdeeds be revealed,
His position could protect them from any charge or incrimination.
So even though Burt and his friends were not known for their brains,
They could fool the Willcox citizens, and turn to robbing trains.

It was the eleventh of September back in eighteen-ninety-nine,
And the boys down at Schwertner's were feeling mighty fine,
As the porter carried drinks to Alvord's party in the smoky back room.
In and out as he carried more,
"There's serious poker goin' on behind that door,"
The busy porter swore to the festive men in the saloon.
As he traded the empties for another tray,
Nobody noticed how he leaned and swayed.
No one suspected just how much that porter had imbibed.
No one was the wiser, no one could have known
That back behind that door he was drinking alone,
Executing Alvord's plan for which he had been bribed.

Everyone saw Alvord's pals go into that room,
But they exited through a window by the light of the moon,
And Stiles and Burts rode hard for the Cochise Station.
Alvord and Downing waited outside of town,
'Til their ears were treated to a distant sound
As their dynamite brought a Wells-Fargo safe to ruination.
Stiles and Burts returned with about thirty grand,
And they entrusted the gold to Alvord's waiting hands,
Then they reconvened at Schwertner's in a state of high elation.

And it wasn't much longer before the news got to town
That the Southern Pacific had been taken down,
And a voice in the crowd said, "We've got to inform the marshal!"
When they entered the saloon they found Alvord and friends
Concentrating on their poker hands,
And drinking whiskey, to which Alvord was partial.

When he heard the news, the sheriff looked shocked,
And he vowed he would scour the canyons.
"I deputize you, and you, and you," he said, pointing to his companions.
And as that posse galloped off, they had to contain their laughter.
The suspects were in custody, but they'd still get away,
Because it was themselves that they were after.

After killing some time the dusty posse returned,
They said the robbers' tracks had mingled with a large horse herd.
They'd all done their duty but the outlaws had still managed to escape.
The deputies all attested to the sheriff's word.
But when someone protested that it sounded absurd,
Burt's normally pleasant grin turned into its opposite shape.
He pounded on the table and made a great show
Of his anger and his frustration.
He claimed that these robbers were the cleverest he'd known
In all the time of his administration.

As the days went by, Alvord felt pleased
That his alibi had proven so successful.
He'd buried the gold in a secret place
So the gang had no choice but to be restful.
His reputation for being short on brains had helped the sheriff put one over,
But he hadn't counted on the tenacity
Of a lawman by the name of Bert Grover.
From the very moment Grover had arrived in town,
Alvord had aroused his suspicion.
Maybe because after the robbers had gotten away,
The sheriff hadn't shown much contrition.
He cajoled the porter from Schwertner's Saloon
Into confessing his role in the plot.
But the waiter didn't wait, and he made his escape
Before charges could be brought.

Meanwhile Alvord and his cronies were feeling confident.
They felt they'd finally found the work for which they'd all been meant.
With Burt's position to protect them they had everything to gain.
The gang was itching to spend their loot,
But Wells Fargo detectives could trace it to its root,
So Burt diverted their attentions to robbing another train.
This time Bob Brown and the Owens brothers
Would be brought on board to assist the others,
But the raid would be led by Bravo Juan and Three-Fingered Jack.
They'd hit the train at the Fairbank station,
And Burt would come up with a fabrication
To cover up their whereabouts until they could get back.

Everything was going according to plan,
And no one found it strange that a Mexican
Would be standing on the platform with four cowboys
Who were noticeably drunk.
But had the outlaws known that in that Express car
A well-known former gunslinger was wearing a star,
Their feelings of bravado would soon have been debunked.
As it was, they got more than they were hoping for
When the Express car pulled up with an open door,
And only one guard who they figured that they'd soon be killin'.
So they opened fire and shot him fast,
But he answered back with a shotgun blast.
For this guard was the legendary gunman named Jeff Milton.

Bravo Juan was hit in the back as he turned to run, abandoning Jack
Whose three fingers were no match for the one on the trigger of a ten-gauge.
Jack's chest caught the force of a mortal wound.
The Owens boys and Brown saw their play was ruined,
So they threw Jack on a horse and fled bloody Milton's rage.
Bravo Juan high-tailed it for Mexico,
And none of them were sorrowful to see him go.
And nobody cares that he hasn't been heard from since.

But the Owens brothers and Bob Brown could see
That Jack's wound made him a liability
If they hoped to escape the law and save their skins.

Jack's wound was bad there was no denyin',
And the boys knew he was beyond their tryin',
So they left him on the Fairbank road just a few miles out of town.
There was no time for Bible verses,
And they spurred their horses to Jack's curses.
They felt sure that he'd expire before the posse came around.
But for once in Jack's life, he found some grit,
And he managed to linger on a bit.
And he was still conscious when the posse came ridin' by.
"They thought they'd get my share of the riches,
But I'll tell you all about those sons of bitches,
And take my revenge on them before I die!"

So Jack fingered all of his fair-weather cronies, giving detailed testimonies
About the failure at Fairbank and the robbery at Cochise.
Alvord and the others maintained their innocence,
But Billy Stiles shattered their smug pretense
When he turned traitor in exchange for his release.
And so it was that Alvord's plans were undone by the shifting sands
And tangled webs of lies and fickle loyalties.
And 'though all the survivors did some time,
No one but Alvord ever saw a dime
Of that for which they'd all given up their lives and liberties.

Alvord came to Willcox one last time when he got out of jail.

He said howdy to his buddies and hung out a few days before he hit the trail.

Burt was a careful poker player. He never showed his hand.

And he just flashed that infectious grin when asked about his plans.

Some old timers like to say

He bought a cattle ranch down in Honduras.

But we long for closure and for certainty, and for morals to reassure us.

Burt Alvord wore a lawman's badge, but it wasn't his truest calling.

And to some of us his betrayal of trust is particularly galling.

There is no record of what happened to the gold, or if it was even mentioned.

But it's hard to imagine Burt coming back around

Without that being his intention.

So whether or not Burt retrieved his hoard is a matter of what one believes.

And there's only one truth left standing here:

There really is no honor among thieves.

A Cowboy Laments the Passing of His Way of Life

The glory days of the American cowboy were embodied by the great cattle drives on the Chisholm, Goodnight-Loving, and Sedalia trails. The assigned roles of the outfit provided stability and discipline while still permitting a man to be an individual operating within a defined code of personal responsibility, camaraderie, and a sense of duty and accomplishment. A man's own skills and work ethic made him a valuable resource to his employer. This of course represents the ideal, but not necessarily the reality. The raucous cattle towns like Abilene, Dodge, Denver, and Cheyenne provided outlets for the release of pent-up emotions and desires. This fostered a feeling of unbridled freedom from the constraints of "normal" lives. Cowboys were poor, hardworking men to be sure, but while in the saddle, out on the trail, they were for all practical purposes the kings of the plains. Their reign was brought to an end by the completion of the great, cross-country railroads and the fencing of the formerly open rangeland. The cattle industry shifted to large ranching operations involving thousands of acres, often owned by consortiums of wealthy mining and railroad magnates and other industry power brokers. Without a wealthy backer, a lone cowboy had little or no chance of buying a ranch and starting his own herd. And even if he did, the economic power of the larger outfits could effectively prevent him from either acquiring necessary supplies or from finding a buyer for his cattle. If a cowboy was fortunate, he might find a place in one of these corporate outfits, but the best he could hope for was to "ride for the brand."

A Cowboy Laments The Passing of His Way of Life

A horse might lame, or die of thirst,
And that "horseless carriage" was the devil's curse,
But the true frontier was brought to a close
By the "iron horse" and the call of gold.
My younger days were wild and free,
My friends and I rode where we pleased.
We spurred and strutted and had our way
With nerves of steel and feet of clay.
But the right to pass is now controlled
By silver tongues and the song of gold.

The wilderness was brought to heel
With iron rails and smoking wheels.
The engine's whistle is a scream of dread.
It smothers my soul like a weight of lead.
The bloodied earth has made me wise.
With the Indians now I empathize.
Fences and towns define trespass.
The mine smokes killed off all the grass.
And all our labor's bought and sold
For loco motives and the lies of gold.

Ridin' to Canyon Diablo

This was actually intended to be song lyrics. Canyon Diablo was a "town" in the loosest sense of the term. To quote former Coconino County sheriff Cecil Calvin Richardson, it was a "mile-long collection of flimsy saloons, gambling halls, and honky-tonks hastily thrown together and vying with one another for the business of the railroad gangs and emigrants on the way west." Together with a few supply stores and Chinese-run restaurants, these occupied the east side of a steep-walled canyon about 35 miles east of Flagstaff. This rough, entrepreneurial assemblage was given its aegis by the Atlantic and Pacific Railroad. Track was laid westward from Winslow, but further construction was blocked by the 250 foot deep and 500 foot wide chasm. Parts of the original bridge were manufactured elsewhere and, when assembled on location, the bridge proved to be several feet short! Bob Thomas claims in a September, 1999 article for Arizona Highways that in the year spanning 1881-1882 more men were killed in Canyon Diablo than the combined death tolls for Tombstone, Dodge City, and Abilene, making it "the West's most deadly town." However, Bob Boze Bell of True West Magazine notes that many authors have repeated exaggerations and fabrications written by Gladwell Richardson (presumably no relation to the C.C. Richardson mentioned above), whose father bought a nearby property called Two Guns in 1950. Apparently Gladwell sought to glamorize the area's reputation for the purpose of enhancing tourism. Whatever its degree of violence and bloodshed, the eventual successful completion of the steel bridge by the Atchison, Topeka and Santa Fe Railroad brought a gasping end to the short life of one of the Wild West's most profligate and dangerous manifestations of "civilization."

Ridin' To Canyon Diablo

Yippee-ky-yi-a! We're ridin' for Canyon Diablo.
Yippee-ky-yi-o! We'll be livin' high tomorrow.

In the middle of hell, at the end of the tracks,
There's a town where the law don't come lookin'.
Just a mile long stretch of whiskey and flesh,
And it's far from your mama's home cookin'.
But you better not go if your gun hand is slow,
Or your lust for blood is wanting.
If you're lacking in nerve, your place is reserved
In the chorus of Boot Hill's haunting.
But there's women and games and a chance to earn fame
By that canyon of the devil.
And there's no guarantees except for the fleas.
And your grave will be rocky and shallow.
Yippee-ky-yi-a! We're ridin' for Canyon Diablo.
Yippee-ky-yi-o! We'll be living high tomorrow.

A boy will stay home, forbidden to roam.
And a young man who yearns for adventure,
Would do well to think twice, when indulging in vice.
He might not live to savor his pleasure.
And a wise man takes care, and offers a prayer
For protection when walking it's alleys.
For the shadows are deep and the price of sin's cheap,
And death waits to add to its tally.
But there's whiskey and games, and a chance to earn fame
By that canyon of the devil.
And there's no guarantees except for the fleas.
And your grave will be unmarked and shallow.

There are those who despise the god-given prize
Of a long life with stretches of boredom.
And some will protest that they can't be their best
If the rest of the world can ignore them.
Some don't have what it takes to deal with mistakes,
And to go on in spite of frustration,
So they trade their soul for a dusty hole
That they fill with a bad reputation.
But there's gold and there's games, and a chance to earn fame
By that canyon of the devil.
And there's no guarantees except for the fleas.
And your grave will be rocky and shallow.

Yippee-ky-yi-a! We're ridin' for Canyon Diablo.
Yippee-ky-yi-o! We might not see tomorrow.
For there's whiskey and games, and women and fame
By that canyon of the devil.
And there's no guarantees except for the fleas.
And your grave will be rocky and shallow.
And your name is forgotten tomorrow.
And your grave will be unmarked…
Yippee-ky-yi-a!

Tuffy's Christmas Ride

Clinton Callaway Peach was the tenth of eleven children born to Alfred and Francis Peach. The family moved to the east fork of the Verde River in 1878, and then to Strawberry (digest that irony!) about 1882. Alfred was instrumental in building the Strawberry Schoolhouse, which the National Registry of Historic Places identifies as Arizona's oldest standing schoolhouse. From the age of two until his death in 1984 (four months shy of his ninetieth birthday), Clinton was known as "Tuffy," a nickname bestowed on him by his elder brother, Hank. As Tuffy described it, "When they sent me to school I could spell T-U-F. So that became my name." When he was twelve years old, an acquaintance gave him a horse, but his father would not allow him to keep it. Tuffy refused to give up the horse, so Alfred turned him out and told him he would have to fend for himself. Tuffy camped in the forest until he was taken in by Prior Miller, his schoolmaster at the Strawberry schoolhouse. At the age of fifteen, Tuffy took the job of mail carrier on the route between Camp Verde and Payson. This was a 104 mile round-trip which was completed every two days, requiring stretches of eleven to eighteen hours in the saddle. A "broomie" was Tuffy's preferred mount for this work. Broomies were ponies with thick hides that were nimble enough to ride through thick brush and under low-hanging branches. Tuffy held the job until the route was discontinued in 1914, making him, in the words of Arizona State Historian Marshall Trimble, "America's last pony express mail carrier." Tuffy also served as State Cattle Inspector for ten years, rode Verde Valley cattle roundups until he was eighty years old, and was instrumental in organizing the Camp Verde Cavalry, which re-enacts the traditions of the Fort Verde Cavalry (1863-1890). From the time I first moved to the Verde Valley, any "old-timer" I met would, upon hearing my name, say, "Why, you must know ol' Tuffy Peach from down in Camp Verde!" But, alas, I never met Tuffy

face-to-face. I have a number of acquaintances and co-workers whose grandparents were friends with him. They have fond childhood memories of Tuffy as a storyteller. The story on which my poem is based was published by Jim Cook (Arizona's self-titled "Official State Liar") on his Journal of Prevarication website, on December 19th, 2007.

Clinton Callaway "Tuffy" Peach, 1966
Photo courtesy Clinton Gray.

Tuffy's Christmas Ride

The sun would soon be setting, so Tuffy had to decide.
The night would be a cold one, and he still had miles to ride.
The track would start to ice up once the light began to fail,
But he'd reached the place where that canyon intersected his trail.
So he paused there for a moment to weigh the pros and cons.
If he had to swim the river in the dark, he'd be soaked to his long johns.
And if he didn't arrive on time, some folks might start to worry,
And organize a search party to set out from Camp Verde.
He'd been in the saddle for hours, and his horse was acting moody,
As if it sensed this side trip was beyond the call of duty.
The broomie stamped and snorted, tossed its head and twitched its tail.
Eager to complete the homeward leg of delivering the mail.
Under such stormy conditions, every minute could prove dear.
But Tuffy knew that if he didn't attempt this,
His conscience wouldn't be clear.

Strapped to Tuffy's bedroll was the source of his consternation –
A package the size of a shoebox that strained his obligations.
In order to obtain this job, he'd lied about his age.
But it soon became more about duty and trust,
Than the one dollar daily wage.
Three times a week he rode his route from Camp Verde to Payson and back.
On his one day off he shod his horse and cleaned and repaired his tack.
And although he was just a teenager, Tuffy did this work with precision.
And this aspect of his work ethic was at the heart of this decision.
If this was any other night, he could just go ahead and leave.
But that package was a present, and this night was Christmas Eve.

The package wasn't very big, but it was loaded with intent.
A woman in Omaha sent it for her bachelor brother, Clint.
'Though he didn't know Clint very well, Tuffy knew that he was a hermit.
And he could get that package through if the weather would only permit.
He knew how lonely it could be to live all by one's self.

His father had thrown him out on his own when he was only twelve.
And he knew that a Christmas package could bring a lot of cheer,
But if it didn't get delivered tonight,
Clint might not come to town 'til next year.

So he turned his horse up the canyon. He was on a Christmas quest.
There'd be no ride tomorrow, so his horse would get some rest.
But the underbrush soon became so thick it was an aggravation.
And when dislodged snow ran down his neck,
He yelled "Thunder and tarnation!"
The canyon quickly narrowed, and the trail became so steep,
That the horse couldn't find its footing because the snow drifts were so deep.
So Tuffy tied him to a tree where he knew that he'd stay put.
The rest of this Christmas mission would have to be made on foot.
His boots were soon soaked clean through
As he trudged through the ice and snow.
And then the frigid water began to numb his toes.
And the package carried in the crook of his arm seemed to double its weight.
And the wisdom of this decision became a subject of debate.
He'd never been to Clint's cabin, only told its approximate location.
And now he was at the mercy of some second-hand information.
The light was growing dimmer and the snow was falling harder.
And Tuffy knew he couldn't afford to go on very much farther.
Could it be that he had bit off more than he could chew?
But just as he began to doubt himself, the cabin came into view.

As he stumbled through the gloom up to Clint's abode,
The last thing he expected to see
Was the note Clint left tacked to the cabin door
That read, "Gone to the country."
Tuffy stood there panting for breath. Everything else seemed hushed.
He felt his heart sink in his chest. He felt his spirit crushed.
He'd thought he could control events and take matters into his own hands.
But it hadn't made any difference to Clint, who was acting on his own plans.

So he turned and staggered down the trail, and climbed back on his horse.
He'd never imagined he could fail, or imagined feeling worse.
He tried to block it from his mind, but one thought would not abate:
"No good deed goes unpunished," and now, thanks to him,
The mail would be late.
But it wasn't his fault that Clint was free
To roam when and where he chooses.
Then he cursed himself because he knew he was only searching for excuses.

As he made his way down off the rim that night,
Toward the twinkling lights of the town,
He thought about how the threads of fate seemed ever so strangely wound.
Tuffy based his identity on this job he'd agreed to do.
And he knew that folks depended on him to get the mail through.
He was young, and it stung him some that he couldn't deliver that present.
But when Clint got around to coming to town,
He'd be in for something pleasant.
When at last he came to the stable, Tuffy sat down on his bunk,
And wrestled into some dry clothes that he kept there in his trunk.
He fed his horse some carrots and began to brush its hide,
When it occurred to him that his disappointment
Was rooted in his own sense of pride.
No path was always easy, and it wouldn't be the last time he'd stumble.
And if he hoped to smooth his way in this world,
It might help if he could be more humble.
Part of what it means to be human is to fall something short of perfection.
And his mood began to brighten in the light of this reflection.
Just then the schoolhouse bell rang out.
The midnight service had concluded.
And it tolled out a blessing for the community,
In which Tuffy was included.
And 'though he'd failed, he now was glad he'd taken that opportunity.
Because delivering the mail plays a vital role in maintaining a sense of unity.
And just like a cowboy needs his horse, people need each other.

No one has all the answers. We are all engaged in wonder.
He'd tried to deliver the sister's gift by the time it was meant to arrive,
But it might mean even more to Clint to receive it at a later time.

It seems that in life, one's joy and one's strife
Are tied to one's own expectations.
So for Tuffy this gift was a chance to come to grips,
And learn to deal with his own frustrations.
No doubt there would often be things in life that he could not control,
But trying to do what he believed to be right would always be his goal.
And he knew to his chagrin that he'd do it all again,
'Though at the moment he felt weak and listless.
In future times of trial he'd strive to go that extra mile.
And he'd do that even if it wasn't Christmas.

The Man Who Killed Santa Claus

This is another true story. My only embellishment is the addition of a few lines of dialogue and of course, the moral at the end. Accounts of this incident can be found in Arizona Highways, in an article by Jack Graham; in Marshall Trimble's Arizona, A Cavalcade of History; and in Shadow of the OhshaD, by Gary Every.

The Man Who Killed Santa Claus

The sense of despair was palpable at the Mesa Merchants' Association.
The Great Depression gripped them in financial strangulation.
The "Roaring Twenties" went out with a snarl,
And one need not look far for the proof.
The economy had gone to the dogs.
The cost of living had gone through the roof.
These were dark days for commerce in 1932.
Now the holidays looked dismal and they didn't know what to do.
Customers were scarce as hen's teeth, and with so many bills to be paid,
They didn't know if they'd be able to hold their annual Christmas parade.

But those who thought debts and creditors
Meant their pageant wasn't meant to be,
Hadn't reckoned on the editor of the Mesa Tribune,
Tenacious John McPhee.
McPhee was a man of spirit, possessed of audacious temerity.
And he was determined to see a return to the days of their former prosperity.
He wasn't one to be constrained by pessimism and negation.
So he wracked his wits and squeezed his brain 'til he had an inspiration.

"I've got an idea – a real blast!" he told the desperate vendors.
"It'll be the salvation of our merchant class,
And motivate those holiday spenders.
It'll grab their attention and make a big splash,"

He told them with conviction.
"And customers will shower you with Christmas cash!"
It was a bold prediction.
"Everyone expects to see Santa Claus
At the head of our Christmas procession.
But the way that I plan to have him arrive
Will make a profound impression.
He won't show up in a car or a sleigh – he'll fall from the sky like snow!
We'll hire a stuntman and an air-o-plane to kick off our Christmas show!
Santa drifts down with a silken cloud billowing high above him,
Waving to the cheering crowd, who've gathered to show they love him.
Then he'll unbuckle his parachute, and as our audience roars,
He'll lead the parade right down Main, directly to your stores!"

The merchants were ecstatic. They heartily endorsed the plan.
Their support was most emphatic. McPhee was a brilliant man!
This skydiving stuntman Santa would have their customers singing.
And the music to accompany them would be cash registers ringing!
McPhee found a willing stuntman, and a contract was arranged.
And by the time he'd rented the plane and the suit,
Everyone's mood had changed.
Gone were the former gloom and doom, the sadness and the grief.
"Happy days are here again!" was everyone's belief.
They could hardly wait for Christmas, and "God bless us, every one!"
The merchants all sang praises for what John McPhee had done.
The excitement was quite tangible. You could feel it in the air.
And they turned their attention to Yuletide décor,
And hung their stockings with care.

Finally came the glorious morning that they'd all anticipated.
As they gathered at the field on the edge of town, everyone was elated.
Children's shining faces, and their parents' smiles were beaming.
Could this be the happy ending of which they'd all been dreaming?
The stores needed a big payday to help meet their bottom line.
They'd been nickeled and dimed since "Black Monday" back in 1929.

The pilot, plane, and stuntman had been no small expense.
But McPhee knew that turning a profit would require some investments.
But as he contemplated how their deficits would shrink,
An assistant whispered in his ear, and his spirits began to sink.
They'd bought into his vision. He'd made them all believe.
But now the stuntman that they'd hired…was absent without leave.
McPhee hadn't thought it was necessary to ask someone to watch him.
But now that it was time to start, it looked like they had lost him!
And as the merchants surrounded him, McPhee knew at a glance
That it had been bad judgment to pay that stuntman in advance.
He quickly dispatched a crew of elves to track the stuntman down,
And as he turned to face the merchants, every one them wore a frown.
"Do not despair. Have faith, my friends," he told the dour shopkeepers.
"We'll find him in some hotel bed. He's one of those late sleepers!"
For several anxious minutes more he strove to calm them down.
Someone muttered, "Tar and feathers, and a rail ride out of town."
And when McPhee said that cooler heads should not jump to conclusions,
They made it clear they'd better hear some plausible solutions.
"You're not a partner in our sorrow. Your job will still be here tomorrow.
Your livelihood's not riding on that flight.
If those customers don't shop our stores,
We're the ones who'll have to close our doors.
You're the only one here with no dog in this fight."
Now an editor needs nerves of steel. He has to be thick-skinned.
And McPhee just wasn't ready yet to throw that white towel in.

Then one of the elves came running up, and from his ashen face,
McPhee got a sinking feeling he was about to be disgraced.
They'd found the wayward stuntman, he hadn't gotten far.
He was plastered to a barstool in a downtown speakeasy bar!
He couldn't stand, he couldn't walk – he couldn't even waddle!
He'd spent the whole night searching for his courage in a bottle.
McPhee could feel the burning stares. Those merchants were seeing red.
So using his most persuasive voice, he turned to them and said:
"I know that things seem bad right now, but we'll salvage a victory.

One of you will just have to play Santa. So who's it going to be?"
But a series of flat refusals soon made things very plain:
McPhee got them into this mess; he was the one to blame.
And since he was responsible for keeping their hopes alive,
He'd be the one to make that jump, and they didn't care if he'd survive.

McPhee felt the noose of failure tightening around his throat.
The merchants now were hopping mad, and he was their scapegoat.
And 'though he was a champion of journalistic might and main,
He knew that he didn't have what it takes to jump from an aeroplane.
But he thought of a way to salvage his plan. He still had one more card.
And now he'd have to play it, or be hoist by his own petard.

"It's always darkest before dawn," he said, "but this is no time for panickin'.
Just bring me an extra Santa suit, and find a department store mannequin.
We'll push the dummy out of the plane
With a static cord attached to the 'chute.
And I'll pop up in the place where it lands, dressed in the second suit.
Then you set off some fireworks, and you begin to shout,
And we'll cover up the dummy and start the parade
Before they figure it out."

The merchants could see that this might be the best chance they would get.
The crowd was growing restless and they'd come too far to quit.
Some dashed off to fetch the props and prepare the plane to scramble.
All their hopes were riding on this dummy Christmas gamble.
And in a while the crowd could hear the airplane's engine sputtering.
And they began to shout and cheer. (The merchants' hearts were fluttering!)
The pilot brought the plane down low to give the audience more,
And to let them see that jolly old elf waving from the door.
They couldn't see the man behind, making the dummy's arm bend,
But they could see that long, white beard, flapping in the wind.
And in the emotion of that moment, the merchants began to bet
They'd pull this stunt off after all. This would be the best Christmas yet!
And now the pilot started his climb, to set up Santa's flight.

And the merchants and everyone else in that crowd
Felt at last things might turn out all right.
And as he watched that plane ascend, McPhee sighed with relief.
For a little while there, the tension was high,
But he'd managed to keep the peace.
They'd overcome great obstacles and done their level best.
Now push that dummy out the door and let gravity do the rest!

And as if in answer to his thoughts, the crowd gave out a cry,
And there was Santa's red-clad form, descending from the sky.
But as they held their gaze aloft, it didn't take them long
To see from the speed he was falling, that something was horribly wrong!
Terror was a frozen mask on every boy and girl.
The 'chute deployed from out of its pack…but it did not unfurl!
Instead of Santa floating down as gently as a feather,
It looked as though both man and 'chute would hit the ground together!
They couldn't tear their eyes away. They wished that they were blind,
As Santa tumbled earthward with that 'chute trailing behind.
What was meant to be inspiring was quickly turning pitiful.
The impact that this stunt would have would tragically be literal.
And when that mannequin smashed to the ground,
The crowd was sickened and silent.
They'd come to see something uplifting.
What they saw was horrific and violent.
The silence was suddenly shattered.
They cried, they gasped,
    and they screamed.
But McPhee still thought he
    could convince them

That it wasn't as bad as it seemed.
He ran out shouting, "Ho, ho, ho!" (You couldn't blame him for trying.)
But the parents were hustling their children away.
His act they were not buying.

The parade went on as scheduled, but it wasn't well attended.
The silence in the stores was deafening. A black cloud had descended.
And in the lonely, deserted aisles, not a creature nor customer stirred.
The shopkeepers' hopes for recovery would have to be deferred.
McPhee laid low for several weeks. He didn't try to be chummy.
His popularity had plummeted along with that department store dummy.
He was *persona non grata*, a notorious Christmas traitor.
He'd dug himself into a hole as deep as Santa's crater.
The quality of dogged tenacity can find a way to spite you.
And even if yours is the hand that feeds, don't think that they won't bite you.
To bank on seasonal goodwill is an ever-present danger.
If expectations aren't fulfilled, you're seen as a dog in the manger.

But time, they say, can heal all wounds, and eventually he was forgiven.
And the citizens turned their attention back to the tasks of everyday livin'.
But even though the memory faded, whenever Christmas rolled around,
McPhee always made up some excuse to get himself out of town.
Anyone can fall from grace, and good things can turn rotten.
But a really bad impression never gets completely forgotten.
McPhee devoted years of service to his community,
But this debacle continued to hound him without immunity.
No matter how much good he tried to do, wherever he would go,
It was always remembered that he was the man
Who put the missile in mistletoe.

It is enough to make one cry to see one's hopes crushed from on high.
And few among us know how bad that feels.
But some of us may feel deprived, and know what it is to live our lives
With regret forever nipping at our heels.
One can atone for hair-brained schemes and try one's best to please,
But if you're going to lie down with dogs,
Don't be surprised if you get up with fleas.
Despite our best intentions, Fate can be cruel and mocking.
Reputation can come crashing down, and coal can fill one's stocking.

They say pride comes before a fall, and disaster awaits the unwary.

And fame can turn into infamy in the words of an obituary.

There were many good and charitable works

For which he might have been known.

But history, it seems, was unwilling to throw McPhee a bone.

Of all the things to be remembered for,

This wasn't what he would have picked.

Some folks say, "Let sleeping dogs lie,"

But one resume credit dogged him even after he died:

He was the guy who devised the demise of Old Saint Nick.

The Story of the 7IL

In May of 2011, I had the opportunity to spend a few days on the 7IL ranch, the only working cattle ranch on the Mojave National Preserve in the Mojave Desert of southern California. This is extremely harsh country and the Blair family, who have ranched there for four generations, must lease 1,000 acres per head of cattle. At the time the ranch had 450,000 acres under lease. The ranch was the focal point of some controversy in the 1990s. The Mojave Desert Tortoise Act required that the habitat of the Mojave Desert tortoise be protected, and it was widely believed by environmentalists that cattle were trampling both the tortoises' burrows and the tortoises themselves. Great pressure was exerted to evict the Blairs and put the ranch out of business. Senator Dianne Feinstein made an official visit to the ranch and came to understand that the case for habitat destruction had been somewhat overstated and, as Rob Blair pointed out, cattle tend to avoid desert tortoises because they are averse to their odor. Additionally, Senator Feinstein realized that evicting the Blairs would put an end to a way of life that had existed in the region for well over 100 years. I have paraphrased her comments in this poem. Rob Blair is himself a well-known cowboy poet and probably the first American to use cowboy poetry in making a case before a United States Senate Committee hearing. By way of a footnote, there are comparatively few agaves growing in that portion of the Mojave Desert occupied by the 7IL, but there are also not very many words which rhyme with Mojave.

The Story of the 7IL

The Mojave's a demanding mistress.
Tough men and women fall under her spell.
It's too harsh a country for the likes of me,
But it's home to the 7IL.
And for the last four generations, determined families of kin
Spend ten hours in the saddle to bring in the cattle.
Then they get up and do it again.

Thousands of people called the valley home
In the days when silver was king.
And the cavalry came to defend the claims

And the white man's vision of things.
And with blood, sweat, and grease, they made a rough peace
With the cactus, the yucca, and the agave.
Then the Civil War came along, and the valley again belonged
To the tortoise, the big horn, and the Mojaves.

John Domingo came to the Fenner Valley to raise his Percheron horses.
He took a chance and established a ranch
Where there was water from dependable sources.
And the old army walls became the stalls in which the herd was stabled.
From the Providence Range to the Colorado River,
The JD ranch was fabled.

When Domingo retired, the first buyer conspired
To turn the ranch for quick profit.
So it fell to J. N. Sanders and his partner "Wash" Gibson
To try to make their living off it.
With the closing of the mines and other signs of the times
The day of the gas engine was at hand.
They felt inclined to bring in bovines, and created the 7IL brand.
Frank Murphy was engaged to manage the range
While the ranch remained in their possession.
Then the partners sold the place to Mark and Mary Pettit
On the eve of the Great Depression.

The Pettits kept the place (with the help of the Craigs) 'til 1934.
And then the ranch passed to E.S. Hass,
Who kept it for four years more.
Two brothers named Herbert and Anson bought it in 1938.
They were the sons of Frank Murphy,
So you could call it a matter of fate.
The Taylor Grazing Act required the brothers to contract
To lease the surrounding public lands.
So from Banshee Canyon to the Clipper Mountains
The range was forced to expand.

Herbert and Anson worked hard to shape
The family's ranching tradition.
And when it came time for them to sell, they made a wise decision.
They sold the place to their nephews, Howard and Jerry Blair.
And now, three generations later, their roots are still buried there.
And now Rob Blair, Howard's son, together with his wife, Kate,
Continue the tradition, and their kids participate.
Lacy, Emily, and Cody have grown up on the 7IL.
Like their parents and grandparents before them,
They're under the Mojave's spell.

Thousands of people worked the valley floor
In the heyday of the Bonanza King.
But what matters now is a thousand acres per cow,
And the water from old Domingo's spring.
The Hunt brothers slammed the door on the quest for that ore,
And the miners haven't been back since.
And the holes they bored stand like open sores on the face of Providence.
And today's not like the good old days.
The world's grown much more cynical.
And the ranching way of life is squeezed in a vise
Between the economic and the political.

When habitat was designated as critical, the Sierra Club voiced its desire.
And seized the hour to brandish its power to hold Congress' feet to the fire.
They marshaled for battle against the grazing of cattle
And the future of ranching looked dire.
The conservationists rallied their supporters
And their voices arose in a chorus:
"The Endangered Species Act says we should take that land back.
Our constituency's aroused because all of those cows
Are trampling on the rights of the tortoise!"

So Rob Blair went before the committee in Washington D.C.
And presented his case that history has its place in exercising democracy.
And he called on the words of another to help make his feelings clear
As he spoke of his home by reciting the poem,
"My Roots Are Buried Here."

But the Sierra Club backed legislation that was powered by public invective.
So the Senator came down and walked the ground,
And it gave her a different perspective.
In the light of her new understanding, she wasn't inclined to rush it.
"Let's balance what we undertake, for there's a way of life at stake,
And we shouldn't be so eager to crush it."
So the 7IL was granted a reprieve, and avoided the bureaucratic fist.
The needs of man were made part of the plan
For cows and tortoises to coexist.

In the hundreds of thousands of acres of the Mojave National Preserve
The 7IL is the only active ranch. A role that it richly deserves.

Now I'm just a chuckline rider, not a cowboy of any degree.
But the thing that I reverence when I'm in its presence is authenticity.
When we stood overlooking the valley,
From the ruins of the old abandoned mine,
And Rob called on his art to bring words from his heart,
He spoke with a passionate pride
Of the spell of the Mojave, and how it made him the man he'd become.
And his words were the kind that fired my mind,
And set me to wonderin' some
About how we're living in dangerous times,
And our country is sorely in need.
But the Blairs' occupation is the backbone of our nation
And thank God they're not the last of their breed.

So no matter your political persuasion,
Whether you're carnivore or vegetarian,
I hope you'll find a similar occasion, to experience a connection to the land.
And whether you're realizing your vision,
Or whether you have drifted from your plan,
And whether you've ever sat on a horse,
I hope you'll recognize the source,
And be reminded what it means to be American.

The Mojave's got a fierce kind of beauty,
'Though it's not the kind of place I'd care to dwell.
But the next time I choose to pull on my boots,
Or the next time I take another bite of steak,
Or the next time I'm raisin' the flag of this nation…
I'll be grateful for the 7IL.

A Bobcat Walked into a Cottonwood Bar

This is a true story. It happened in March of 2009, and the video footage can be viewed on YouTube. The story was covered by news media across the nation. I have never spoken with any of the people who were in the bar on that night, so in taking some poetic license with this piece, I may have veered somewhat from the truth in stating that Derrick hadn't ever given any consideration to the idea of human and animal interactions. Maybe he had, and I suspect he certainly must have done so since. Nor do I know if he has fathered any children. I also do not know if the bartender actually wears bifocals, but I needed a rhyme for "locals" ("yokels" was out of the question). Additionally, I have never had any involvement with prostitution and mean no disrespect to the various communities mentioned. I also do not mean to make light of the tragedies involving Siegfried and Roy or the late Steve Irwin, but as the saying goes, "if you play with fire you are going to get burned." Satire is not for the squeamish, and my admonition about wildlife's place in our world reflects my true personal feelings on the matter. Lastly, the song titles mentioned are in no way a reflection of my political beliefs or affiliations.

During one of my shows at the Sedona Heritage Museum in 2010, I noticed that when I introduced and began performing this poem, the members of a family in attendance got particularly excited, the father and children turning and grinning at the mother, who also seemed to find a special enjoyment in this piece. After the show, they came up and she introduced herself as an emergency room nurse from the Verde Valley Medical Center, where the victims were treated following the incident. She told me she had treated two of the cat's three victims on that night, and that they had originally given her a very different accounting of how they had come by their wounds, but by the time they returned for subsequent rabies treatments the story had gone viral, and they sheepishly admitted the truth. The Chaparral Bar in Cottonwood has profited from its notoriety by selling a tee-shirt that sports a lewd interpretation of the incident.

A Bobcat Walked into a Cottonwood Bar

A bobcat walked into a Cottonwood bar - possibly in search of a punchline.
And what happened after would generate laughter
And hours of internet fun time.

It was quiet that night, and the usual suspects
Were holding their barstools down
In the comfortable dark of the Chaparral Bar
On the highway that runs through Old Town.

Bartender Scott had just bid goodnight to some of the customary locals,
When they tumbled back in through the still-open door,
And darn near knocked off his bi-focals.
And hot on their heels was one pissed-off bobcat –
About 30 pounds of feline fury.
He'd already left one victim bleeding in the Pizza Hut lot
When he staggered in, all matted and furry.
Some leapt for the tables, others dove for the bar,
Some stood frozen like statues of granite.
As that frazzled cat blearily assessed the scene,
Like a bad out-take from Animal Planet.

Now Kyle had been drinkin', so we might just excuse
His apparent situational blindness.
Maybe he thought the foam flecked 'round that cat's mouth
Was the milk of human kindness?
But he'd soon have good reason to later regret
That he hadn't stayed home in his pajamas
When his spontaneous audition for a Darwin Award
Was caught by the security cameras.
In spite of Scott's warnings, Kyle knelt down
Inserting himself into the equation.
But when he pulled out his cell phone to photograph the cat,
He got a face-full of cuts and abrasions.

As the cat next closed in on a couple of ladies,
Derek jumped up and pushed them aside.
But when that cat started climbing up the leg of his pants,
He had to salvage his manly pride.
When it comes to survival of the fittest,
Men can easily be made to look like fools.
But when a wildcat's shredding your best pair of Wranglers,
You've got to try to save your jewels.
Before that night Derek never gave a thought
To questions of inter-species exploitation.
And although the cat extracted a pound of his flesh,
He's still a candidate for procreation.

Then that bad cat dashed back out into the night,
After having behaved so dastardly.
And it's a fair assessment to say that that bar,
Had been the scene of a bona-fide cat-astrophe.
The word Scott would use when later interviewed was "pandemonium",
But given the evidence on the videotape,
He might have said just plain "dumb".
Some men spend their whole lives seeking fame,
Others have it thrust upon them.
Kyle and Derek were cat-apulted onto the national stage
With the smell of cat pee on them.

But the cat-alog of that cat's misdeeds was about to come to an end.
As he cat-erwauled from his cat-bird seat,
Cottonwood cops came round the bend.
And when he charged they drew their guns, and blew away all nine lives.
'Cause there's more than one way to skin a cat,
And the heavily armed will survive.
No one knows what made that cat mad,
Or set it on its quest for guts and glory.
But it's misadventures in the bar that night
Surely ranked in a criminal cat-egory.

So let's take a lesson from Siegfried and Roy,
And remember what happened to Steve Irwin.
Wildlife wasn't put on this earth to be our toy, of that you can be certain.
And if there is a cosmic soundtrack to our lives,
It would make me a true believer,
If the music that was playin' on that bar's jukebox,
Was Stray Cat Blues, or maybe Cat Scratch Fever.

So tomcats be advised, if you're lookin' for a rise,
You might check out the cat houses of Jerome.
And up in Flagstaff you can always find some laughs
If you're lookin' for love far from home.
And you can get down and dirty in Sedona or Camp Verde,
If you've got the cash and the endurance.
But if you're tryin' to score some goods in the town of Cottonwood,
You'd better be paid up on your insurance.
So do your cattin' around in some other town,
No ifs, ands, buts, or maybes.
Because that kitty at the bar, she can scratch and she can scar.
And there's a pretty decent chance she could have rabies!

The Killing of Sedona Sue

In 1984, a local newspaper solicited poems about Sedona written by local residents and visitors. Doubtless they expected an outpouring of highly emotional sentiments praising the scenic splendor and affirming the enlightened nature of those of us who were wise enough to discover our destinies enshrined by these sacred cliffs. But my early Sedona experiences had acquainted me with a peculiar brand of arrogance which seemed to possess some red rock residents. Interestingly, it seemed more prevalent in some of the newest residents rather than among those whose forebears had settled here before the place was completely "civilized." It was a certain lack of humility, as if they felt they were somehow spiritually superior by virtue of living in the midst of such natural beauty. (One can still encounter this attitude.) So rather than babble about the bliss induced by Oak Creek's burbling waters or the serenity of meditating at a positive vortex, I chose to take a different approach. Knowing that the Oak Creek Tavern had been the place of the founding of the Cowboy Artists of America, I envisioned it as the location for a very different kind of scene, populated by various local "characters" named for towns in the Verde Valley and surrounding environs. For inspiration I borrowed heavily from Robert W. Service's "The Shooting of Dan McGrew," so if you are hearing a sound in the background while you read this, it might well be him turning over in his grave. Needless to say, my entry in the paper's contest was not deemed worthy of printing (some people just don't understand satire), but it has become something of a "cult favorite" and is frequently requested at many of my appearances.

The Killing of Sedona Sue (Redux)
(With apologies to Robert W. Service)

A bunch of the gals were holding the fort at that old Oak Creek Saloon.

They were killing the chill by drinking their fill,

And kicking the dented spittoon.

Down one end of the bar an exhibition of scars

Was being given by Montezuma Mary,

And by Red Rock Ruth, who was more uncouth,

'Though her legs were a trifle less hairy.

Jerome Jeanette danced a minuet,
Then arm-wrassled with Flagstaff Florrie,
While Verde Val, their voluptuous pal,
Choked on her own sob story.
There was Tuzigoot Tess (she had settled for less),
She was boasting of men she had known,
As Cottonwood Connie, just to be on'ry,
Gave out with a lecherous groan.
Clarkdale Charlotte, the notorious harlot, was locked in a heated exchange
With Cornville Lenore, who's as at home on a floor
As anywhere else on the range.
Pretty Prescott Priscilla, who reeked of vanilla,
Was guzzling beer out of her shoe.
And sucking down gin like a veteran of sin, sat surly Sedona Sue.

She was dealing the cards to her local pards.
She was picking their pocketbooks clean.
And helping her cheat was her current sweet, a skinny kid known as Dean.
He had a thin mustache, and it gave him some sass,
As well as first prize there, I reckoned,
Of any mug in the place that grew hair out its face,
('Though a couple gals came in close second!)

When out of the dark of the high desert night,
A stranger crashed in on the boredom.
And those local dears gave with catcalls and jeers,
But she stood there and calmly ignored 'em.
She had a spark, and it set her apart
From the hustlers, and the barflies, and the nighthawks,
And the rest of the slime that crawl in to kill time
And avoid rolling up with the sidewalks.

As she made for the bar like a railroad car
Someone called, "Who invited this strumpet?"
But she set down a sack she'd had slung 'cross her back,
And pulled out a battered old trumpet.
And a hush fell over the crowded room,
'Though the stranger remained serene.
But I chanced to glance, and I saw that he'd blanched,
That skinny kid known as Dean.
As she raised that horn to her puckered lips, puffed out her cheeks and blew,
"Our next game'll be straight Chump Change," said surly Sedona Sue.

Then that tin antique gave out with a squeak!
It was long, it was lean, almost deadly!
But she cut off its climb with some classic ragtime,
Then broke into a big band medley.
Through the smoke and the noise she maintained a poise
That no one in that crowd could subvert.
Then she made a sudden shift to an improvised riff
In the Dixieland style of Al Hirt.
But that kid named Dean, it was almost obscene
How his ears seemed on fire from her arson,
As she blew it out wild in a Hollywood style,
Like Doc Severenson used to on Carson.
The music was hyperbolic and my mood turned melancholic
With more alcoholic ingestion.
And a sense of doom suffused the room
Until reality itself seemed in question.
Was I being deceived by what I perceived?
Or was my memory being too frugal?
Did she express her regret on a coronet?
Or was she wailing away on a bugal?
As she turned it about, and mellowed it out
With something by Chuck Mangione,
Something about Sue I began to see through –
Something deceitful and phony.

Then the trumpeter's set got as loud as it gets,
But she seemed restless and forlorn.
She played Herb Alpert 'til my eardrums hurt
As notes flew like bullets from that horn.
With each song she commenced I became more convinced
Of that music's destructive potential.
And it seemed that its goal was to capture my soul
In a dread dark and existential.

My next view of Sedona Sue showed a face like a mask of malice,
As the hot room swooned, and that trumpet crooned out a tune
By Winton Marsalis.
Then a thought I can't explain popped into my brain.
Had it entered there by osmosis?
Maybe it was the vodka, but I was thinking about Kafka
And that story he called Metamorphosis.
There was a peculiar flavor to the stranger's behavior,
And frankly it was starting to bug me.
I became obsessed with how her music would caress,
And then turn around and slap me, or drug me.

Then the stranger called, "Last song!" And played Louie Armstrong.
Man, she blew it out Bourbon Street big!
She attacked her last chorus with a bodacious force
That blew off Sedona Sue's wig!
Then she lowered that horn from her blistered lips,
(One of which I noticed was bleedin').
And she glared at Sue, but addressed her as "Steve"!
And asked, "How'd it go over in Sweden?"
Then someone screamed, and the lights went out,
And two bodies clashed in the night.
And what we beheld when the lights came up was not a pretty sight.
The stranger lay dead from a blow to her head.
Her trumpet lay broken in two.
But cut to the bone – and the silicone! – lay surly Sedona "Sue"!?!

This is the way it all went down, as near as I can tell.
I don't know much 'bout transgender and such,
And I guess that's just as well.
They say that all's fair in love and war. They say that revenge is sweet.
They say that you never really know someone
'Til their shoes are on your feet.
They say that the stranger was out of her mind,
But nobody saw what I seen –
The fella that kissed her – and made off with that horn –
Was that skinny kid known as Dean.

The Cactus Killer (A Tale of Murder and Revenge)

The events described in this poem are true. They took place on February 4, 1982, in the desert outside of Phoenix. My idea for Nature's condemnation of the dead man was inspired by orations made by Judge Roy Bean, the self-styled "law west of the Pecos", Judge Isaac Parker, the so-called "hanging judge" of Fort Smith, Arkansas, and Judge Kirby Benedict of Taos, New Mexico, a personal friend of Abraham Lincoln. Omar S. Barker of the Western Writers of America quotes these orations in his chapter "Rhetoric from the Bench" in Legends and Tales of the Old West. It is interesting that all three of the cases from which Mr. Barker quotes these words involved Mexican defendants. It makes one wonder whether these judges resorted to such "high toned" language when sentencing Anglo defendants. Perhaps it was a way of establishing the court's authority to impose the ultimate penalty on these outlaws. Another interesting point is that all three of these orations are strongly reminiscent of each other. I suppose it's possible that newspaper accounts might have featured the text of one or more of these speeches, which in turn might have been studied by one or the other of these judges. These three speeches also have something else in common. They all call to mind the lyrics of the song sung by the spirit Ariel in Shakespeare's "The Tempest." ("Full fathom five thy father lies; Of his bones are corals made; Those are pearls that were his eyes...") Shakespeare's plays were very popular in nineteenth century America, and traveling productions visited some of the wildest of western towns. Perhaps one or more of these judges obtained their inspiration for such lofty language by attending some of these performances.

In the "it's a small world" department, after giving a training on saguaro cactus in 2012 in which I made mention of this incident, one of my co-workers told me that he had been a member of the search and rescue team that found the body of the shooter. He said they'd ridden past it a few times before finally spotting only the finger tips of one of his hands protruding out from underneath the cactus, the rest of his body being thoroughly covered by the bulk of his victim.

The Cactus Killer
A Tale of Murder and Revenge

A young man with a shotgun was seeking recreation,
So he drove out to the desert to wreak some devastation.
And there he looked for a target suitable for his practice,
And he set his sights on bringing down a giant saguaro cactus.
No one knows what made him choose this cactus for his victim.
Maybe as he passed close to it, it had the nerve to prick him?
Maybe it was the tallest and it stood out from afar?
Maybe it was just the closest one to where he'd parked his car.

The gunman wouldn't have described himself as being a home-wrecker,
But that cactus was home to a family of owls and a Gila woodpecker.
It's certain that he didn't ask, but if that saguaro could talk,
It might have said it was the favorite perch for a local Harris' hawk.
"It's only a plant," was all that he thought before deciding to shoot.
Now the Tohono O'odham people will miss collecting its fruit.

So he pumped a shell into the chamber, and blasted away at its flesh.
But the giant stood undaunted. It wasn't much impressed.
Its cells must surely have felt some pain from this obscenity,
But it had withstood sun, and wind, and rain for more than a century.
Impervious stood the giant, 'though some of its ribs were exposed,
As if refusing to acknowledge the damage its attacker had imposed.
So as if it was the enemy in his own personal war,
He kept repeating the process, and pumped in several more.
By now it'd got his dander up, and he started to cuss and rant.
He wasn't going to be shown up by a stupid, gol-darned plant!
So again he fired, and again and again, 'til he'd used up his ammunition.
That cactus wasn't going to defeat him.
Its downfall had become his mission.
He ripped out a section from its broken ribs, and swung it like an axe.
He knew it had to topple from the force of his attacks.
Man has dominion over nature. How dare it continue to stand?

Then he paused to pull a splinter from his red and throbbing hand.
There was a subtle cracking sound, and then a sudden "whoosh!"
And the last thing he saw was the consequence of a universal truth.
Energy involves mass and speed, as Einstein formulated.
But three thousand pounds plus gravity was unanticipated.
When the victim struck its attacker, the ground beneath them shivered.
And the attacker's life was extinguished by the force these facts delivered.

You could call this murder and revenge. but you couldn't call it sport.
And swift is the karmic justice that is dealt in Nature's court.
And when the dust had settled, and silence reigned again,
One could almost imagine Nature's voice floating on the wind.
And if the killer yet could hear, 'though his pain would've been intense,
These words brushing against his ears would have described his sentence:

"The winter shall give way to spring;
The flowers will bloom, the birds will sing,
But you'll not hear their joyful songs as you lie paying for your wrongs.
The summer next will have its sway; cicadas will buzz, and lizards play,
But for you these things will come too late, as your tissues desiccate.
Next in its turn will come the fall with sunset colors to enthrall,
But you'll not smell the cooling rain
That washes the sand your blood has stained.
The winter next completes the wheel as vultures above you dance and reel
On the arid wind that keens and moans
Among the gaps between your bones.
No more for you are laughter and mirth
As your victim pins you now to earth.
What is given to you is what you gave.
Two skeletons now shall mark your grave."

Some believe that from God's hand the earth was given unto man.
But even if that is the truth, it gives no license for abuse.
Man does not inhabit this world alone,
And other lives have needs of their own.

Worthy stewards and guardians don't scar the landscape with their sins.
We claim the right of exploitation but exceed the limits of regeneration.
The earth would be within its rights to cleanse itself of such parasites,
And take whatever revenge it can for crimes committed by the hand of man.
But if these ideas meet with your rejection…remember:
God gave the cactus needles for its own protection.

www.ingramcontent.com/pod-product-compliance
Lightning Source LLC
Chambersburg PA
CBHW080747250626
47162CB00010B/3051